# Divine Justice:
# The Creation

By

# George Karavidas, G.K.

Argus Enterprises International
New Jersey***North Carolina

A-Argus Better Book Publishers, LLC

For information:
A-Argus Better Book Publishers, LLC
9001 Ridge Hill Street
Kernersville, North Carolina 27285
www.a-argusbooks.com

ISBN: 978-0-615672-5-7
ISBN:  0-615672-5-7


Book Cover designed by Dubya

Printed in the United States of America

# DEDICATION

To my 11 year old Daughter Elena, where although she came a bit late into my life, gave me joy and meaning I never experienced before. By the looks of it, she is following my footsteps.

In addition: To those children they have to tear their hearts apart, by their divorced Parents.

# INTRODUCTION

`Dear Reader! Since September 11 2001, where thousands of innocent people lost their lives with the cruelest manner, I decided to devote my life to reduce and eventually eliminate terror as it manifests.

One of my efforts, is this Fiction Book that you have in your hands, call `Divine Justice The Creation`, I wish in time to make it a movie (Serial)`

A new Hero is just born; with all the trimmings of the modern Technology, but with a unique Ancient Greek background.

His realistic fighting movements will be easy to understand by the Reader, because of the many years of experience in Martial Arts by the Author (Look at the back pages of the book).

The main Hero, although the most skillful in Fighting Combat, not only will never retaliate with a crime, but at all times will maintain and be an example of perfection of character and discipline, with respect to the Older, the Weak and to Children...

Certainly will punish those deserve, but with his unique way!

Possible he resembles the looks of Robin Hood and Batman. Could be close and a head of the Geniuses mind of James Bond. But very soon, You, the Reader, will realize that he Copies, No One!

What makes him to be Genuine and will make You, to be proud of being your Hero, is apart of the way he handles every situation; how he punishes the bad ones or the bad ones, or how he saves the weak and makes them friends for life etc…is because of the way he was brought up…

The Story is geared not only for the young boys and girls where they have their roots deep into their Families, but to every Young Adult.

This kind of a young man though, is of a bright example to us all!

Into his effort to fight crime, he will not be alone, as it will be a Family affair, thus, in this way, the Whole Family can read it!

In this book and the others to come, you will experience the appearances of Goddess Athena, which in Ancient times was the Protector of War and of the Family.

This is a fiction story, where although will have really happenings in it, by bringing Goddess Athena, or possible some Spirits of the Ancient Era, it doesn't mean that the Writer is going `Nuts` or against any Religions, as he is a Religious man himself.

Also, you will be surprise to learn few things about the Ancient Olympic Champions and their Gymnasts, of how ahead they were in all Spheres (Even of our time), concerning the Athlete, the Athlete's need; regarding Medicine, Psychology etc.

One of the Ancient Greek Writers call, Lukianos; writes that:

`The First Gymnast was God Hermes, and his first Athlete - Student was also a God, call, Prometheus`

On the other hand: It was written and it's saved, at the Holy Mountain of Athos, that, Ancient Philosophers such us: `Socrates and Solon, were predicting the coming of Jesus Christ to Earth`

At all times, the Author will be together with you and will give you answers before you develop any questions…`

*Devine Justice: The Creation*

## CHAPTER ONE

A bus full of children is moving through the National road with the Mountain Olympus (Height 2917 meters) as its final destination.

The children, Girls and Boys, about 40 in numbers and between the ages of 6 to 15 years old, are singing camping songs.

If one could listen to them and analyze their voices, would feel that most of these children were not carefree as any child should be, but worried and insecure for their future. The reason was, that they were orphans and alone in this cruel World, without a Home and Parents to support and love them, to share the warmth and the security of the Family.

The staff of the Orphanage, organized this trip to Mount Olympus `B` Section, call `Little Water Taps` with height of 1800 meters, for the children some time ago, and the − day, Saturday 15th of June 1983, become a reality.

As the bus moves at low speed through the National road towards the Mount Olympus, one of the three Teachers accompanied the children, realized of what happened and started a new song, hopping to give them some joy…

Some of them were following her from the start, but gradually the others were picking up as well.

It appears, that all the Kids are enjoying the new song and giving a picture of join - in with their Teacher, but in case someone could take a stroll inside the bus, would see things differently, as out of the 40 children (26 boys and 14 girls), we see that 11 of them are not singing at all.

Let's take a good look at a 12 - year old, Mediterranean - looking boy, where he sits alone at the back seat of the bus, looking through the window.

He is not singing. In fact, mentally, he is not there at all! His eyes are focused at the valley below, much lower than the height of the Mountain.

As we come closed we see him moving his head directing his eyes towards Olympus, but again 'He is not there'.

He looks sad and at this very moment few tears are coming out of his brown eyes. Quickly he takes a handkerchief from his pocket and wipes them off. We look in surprise that his wristwatch is very expensive. Actually is a genuine Rolex! His handkerchief has the initials, of G.K...

Before we live him to move farther down, we also noticed that he holds within his left hand (On the empty seat next to him) a stick, attached to a net. In fact, it is a 'Butterfly Net Catcher'.

As we move towards the driver of the bus; two children, appears to be Brother and Sister, about the same age as G.K., are holding hands and instead of singing or at least looking out of the window, they are crying.

Inside their hands, they are holding a photo. This is a photo of their parents and themselves, hanging each other happily...

The Bus finally reached its destination, which is, Olympus B - Section.

They parked the Bus into the area where visitors were permitted to stop when visiting the National Park.

The children speedily disembark with their Teacher – Warden, Mrs. Maria, where she gives them instructions of not to wander far a way as they had to walk to their

Bungalows for their 2 day visit to the Mountain of the Ancient Greek Gods.

The view of Mount Olympus towards the Valley bellow was breath taking, but G.K. our little Mediterranean boy, had a different idea about the view as he moved away of the group and run after a… butterfly.

He was holding the stick of the Butterfly Catcher (Where by now he had it extended to a good measurement of about 3 feet - long) above his head with his right arm, and the net fully open, ready to cutch the innocent insect with its colorful winds… ignoring the warning of his Teacher of not to get a way from the Bus.

While running after the Butterfly, he kicks whatever he finds in front of him mainly bushes and loose Rocks. Every time when he tries to trap the Butterfly, you can see that he moves with speed and grace, like a young cat, with excellent balance.

In case someone had Martial Arts background, could sworn that the boy is a young Martial Artists and a very talented one, as he takes a `Stand` after every move he makes, with his net up in front of his body on one hand and a close fist on the other, like he is facing an adversary or an animal, ready to fight.

While he is enjoying running after the B/fly he is also getting away from the Bus.

Eventually he managed to cutch it with his net by a sharp movement of his hand.

With the greatest of care, he places the stick on the bushy ground; also he is placing slow his foot over the stick, thus by now he has both his hands free.

With his left hand he lifts the one side of the net and with the other hand takes the delegate Butterfly using only his two fingers (His thump and index). Very gently and very slowly brings it in front of his face.

While he examines it, he talks to it:

"You are one of the 15 000 species of Lepidopteron... oh well; if I had my book that I left it in the Bus, I could tell you exactly of what kind you are. Anyway, you are so beautiful it would be pity to keep you prisoner."

While shaking his head, carries on talking:

"I know what is like to be alone with out a Family. You are lucky though that you can fly..."

With a sharp movement of both his hands, he sets the B/fly free.

While he is watching it flying away, he sits on a little rock and carries on talking to it:

"Oh, I wish I could fly like you, to visit far away places and learn everything about Martial Arts from the Great Masters of the world. I want to be like them and..."

Suddenly... he is interrupted by a strange voice that could come from a Man, who tells him...

"Follow me!" "Follow me!"

The little boy gets up and looks around, seeking out the strange voice, but he sees nobody. With out thinking he moves towards the voice where keeps telling him the words... "Follow me".

The voice, although at some distance, sounds like it belong to an old man but he cannot see him.

All of a sudden he sees in the woods, the back of a very old man with white hair and white long beard, dressed in a white robe. The old man, while he is walking away from the boy, looks like he is not touching the ground. He turns his head back and tells the boy the same words "Follow me"... and as he came out of nowhere, he disappears in the woods.

The boy moves slowly forward and grasps his net in front of his body. He is surprised but not afraid.

He stops, and looks around for the old man... then... suddenly the earth tremors and the ground opens. The clean blue sky becomes full of whirlwind white and black clouds. The boy is lifted from the ground, while dropping his net, he spins around and around, going into colorful channels, spinning and tossing, turning over and over... until finally he faints.

# CHAPTER TWO

When he awakes, he finds himself on the floor of a large Cave with very little lighting. He gets to his feet and assumes a fighting stance with his fists closed in front of his body. Like a Boxer facing an opponent.

He looks around and gapes in surprise, as he is in the center of a very large round theatre -like. There are 12 wooden hand - carved desks, where behind them are 11 men seated, with one empty. He cannot see their faces as there is not enough light, but he can see clearly their dresses where are of the Ancient Athletes.

On top of their heads, they are wearing a wreath… he cannot believe it… as these Athletes, are Ancient Olympic Winners, and they have being awarded the `Kotinos`(The Olympic Wreath), for capturing first place in their sport.

Please note: In the Ancient Olympics, there weren't second and third places, only First.

His thoughts are interrupted by a very commanding sharp voice:

"Little boy, look around you carefully, for what you see are the Spirits of the best Ancient Greek Gymnasts, for Boxing, Wrestling and Pagratio.

All of them were Olympic Champions in the Ancient Olympics, became the best Masters of all time. They devoted their lives in what they believed to be as the best Fighting Art. They have exercised their minds and body to that extent, thus, achieved the ultimate of their Art. They were legends of their time. These Spirits brought to you to give you what you most desire, but I will command them to teach you, one Master-Spirit at a time.

The learning period with them will be 10 years."

The voice carries on:

"The empty seat is reserved for the Master that is still alive. He is also Greek and he is well known in the Martial Arts world. He is very strict and will drive you to the limits. Although he has no mercy for those who violate the Law, he is very soft and kind, especially to children, as he has none of his own. With him, you will be practicing for the rest of his life, as he will make you his successor to his Unique Fighting Art that he has created. When the time comes, you will learn whom he really is!"

While trying to see the names of those seated, the little boy shakes his head left - right, because he doesn't see names, but only the sport they were doing.

He managed to read and find out that they were: 5 Pagration, 3 Boxing and 3 Wrestling. All Olympic Champions, winners of their sport!

Please note: Pagratio was a combination of boxing and wrestling, started in 648 b. C. (Please look at the back of the book).

After looking through all their faces, he looks around, seeking the voice that commanded him about his future.

As he can't see anybody, he asks the strange voice while makes an effort not to tremble:

"What kind of power you have when you a Woman... that can bring to life the Spirits of all these dead Ancient Legends where are all Men?"

After few seconds of silence, a bright light envelops the boy.

The light now is moving towards the top of the cave and in front of the boy's eyes, a giant woman dressed in Ancient war Armour, holding on one hand a shield and on the other a spear, while on her head she is wearing an Ancient Helmet, appears.

The boy, after carefully study the woman, he realized who she was ... His mouth was moving but his voice barely came out.

Eventually he listens to himself saying:

"ATHENA! The Ancient Goddess of Wisdom, Protector of Family and of War..."

While he is saying these words, he drops to his knees, and continues talking to the Goddess:

"You and this place... I have seen it in my dreams, almost every night for the past two years! You brought the old man to Olympus. You brought me here!"

The Goddess confirms his words and commands him to promise to her that he would devote his life and apart of learning from all those Legends, he in return will use his knowledge for the cause of Justice, wherever needed, not only in Hellas (Greece) but also in all 5 Continents.

"You must obey the Laws! But be merciless to the bad ones. Protect the Weak and the Innocent. Fight crime at all costs, but with out been a murderer your self! Be the `Justice` but not the `Jury`."

The Goddess continues by saying:

"The entire Ancient Master - Spirits, will teach you Philosophy and Natural Medicine.

The living Master will teach you apart of his Fighting Art also Modern Science and Technology. Do not forget, that you are Greek and you have a colorful history of being part of the first Democratic Nation, we spread our Civilization through Alexander the Great into most Countries...

**11**

Later on, through you, the modern World will learn the importance to be JUSTICE! Now give me your word and swear that you will fulfill and obey my commands"

The boy gets up and looks straight to the Giant Goddess, trying to penetrate the strong light that envelops her.

With out thinking, he lifts both his hands up, stretching his open palms and bows to her, while replies with tears in his dark brown eyes:

"I swear Goddess Athena I swear!"

Please note: This kind of a bow, years later, became the symbol of respect, between Teacher and Students…

## CHAPTER THREE
### 21 Years later

A convertible motor - car drives smoothly towards the Mound Olympus.

Behind the wheel is a reasonable young man wearing Sunglasses. His looks are of Mediterranean background. His age can be something between 30 to 35 years, medium height, with a very serious looking face.

When memories floods his thoughts and unfolded in side his mind while he is enjoying the scenery of the surroundings, then, his face becomes younger as he smiles. But when his face gets heard and looks older is when he is thinking of something that it's not so much worth of smiling.

These two quick sentimental changes in a human, indicates a very intelligent and yet a very mind-free young man...

This time of the year, where spring hangs on for another 15 days (It is 15th May 2006), before pass it on to summer, makes the sides of the road very colorful. The wild flowers are blossomed and they look so much alive... but the driver of the convertible car, although looks at the flowers while he drives carefully the up hill road, he is in a hurry to reach his destination...

Eventually he arrives at the parking area, especially made for the visitors who wanted to visit that particular part of Mt. Olympus, which is the B section call Vrisoules (Little water taps).

He gets out of the car and he sighs at the beauty of the surroundings.

He observes another two cars parked further down. He looks around to find the owners of the cars, but sees nobody. In his mind, he stores both cars number plates.

As he takes off his light blue sunglasses, unveils a small scar at the end of his left eye.

While looking around, he decides to take a walk to a path towards the woods, leaving the windows of his car open, but places the roof top cover.

While walking slowly, he examines from time to time the area like he is looking for something. A smile comes out of his face when he sees a little rock. He placed his palm on it and memories are coming clean in his mind, makes him smiling again. He carries on walking further and looks around more carefully then before. He moves some bushes with his hands, glancing around, then turns left and after a bent turns to the right…

He looks in side a thick bush and eventually he finds what appears to be a little net attached to a stick, to catch Butterfly's with it. He smiles instantly with happiness like a little child who finds his lost toy.

While he examines it, the net itself is no longer intact as time had almost destroyed, but memories returned again. His expressions are mixed as he remembers more and more.

After few seconds pasted, the man raises his head towards the blue sky and talks to it:

"Goddess Athena! I know that you are here. Twenty - one years had past since you gave me your commands. I have learned and practice with mind and body, suffering torture, to fulfill my promise. Now I am ready physically and mentally to take the road that I swore on oath to you, and…"

His voice suddenly interrupted by a thunder from the sky, followed up by… a scream from the parking area…

The voice calling for help, looks like belongs to a young Girl!

Without hesitation, he turns and run towards the parking area.

When comes out of the woods he throws the net in his car through the open window and continues running.

He stops at an opening between trees and of what he sees made the normally calm face to become hard as granite.

A young girl of about nineteen years old, is held from her two arms by two men where are pulling her viciously whilst she screams. They are dragging her towards a car that is parked near by.

The scream is stopped by a hard smack on her face from one of the men...

Further on at his left side, he sees another two men who are fighting in a strange manner. One is telling the other that he is going to punching him to his face. At his command, the `adversary` stretches his jaw forward, while looking at his left to see if somebody is watching them.

The first man, with out hesitation, punches him with his right arm, making no damage at all. In fact, he is not even touched him!

The funny attacker, during this funny performance, he shouts loudly, like he is a Karate expert, punching his opponent in competition.

G.K. (Now a full grown up man) saw clearly that the whole setup was badly directed and acted.

As the punched man falls on the ground, thus, dirty his expensive summer clothes, he screaming, pretending he got hurt.

The attacker follows by a kick to the ribs with his right leg, again without harming him; both screaming, with one pretending to be in pain, and the other to be in anger.

G.K. shaking his head left - right with a disgrace…but, as right now he had no time and reason to solve this far – fetched puzzle…

He looks at the other side and… without any hesitation he runs towards the two men telling them to leave the girl alone.

The distance now is about 3 meters. He is using words to insult them by calling them "Animals."

The two men glance at each other and like as they were reading each other's mind, throw the girl to the ground and attacked him.

Both, while running towards him, they look very funny as they try to appear wild and angry, making some funny noises inside their ugly mouth.

G.K. waits until they are close and when the one at his left tries to kick him with his right leg (Front kick) then, G.K. slides his body to the left and blocs the leg with his right arm. He does the block with a perfect side stance; followed by lifting his right leg and kicks the assailant behind his knee. The force is hard, that drives both the thug's knee on the ground breaking it. By keeping his kicking leg behind the damaged knee, he follows a strike with his left open palm (Palm hill strike) on to his right ear, making the screaming to stop and sends him to the ground unconscious.

Before the thug hits the ground, G.K. releases his kicking leg, places it on the ground and by sliding it to his right side kicks the second villain with a sidekick to his Solar plexus. The kick is so powerful that lifts the shocking man of the ground, breaking some ribs and sends him to sleep, following his partner on the hard tar ground.

He looks at the girl where by now she is getting herself up, dusting her jean and her blouse… G.K. cannot help admiring her magnificent body…

He turns his face to the other side, to see the outcome of the mysterious set up…

Not surprised he sees the one who beats the other, coming towards him, with his fists in front of his body, swearing in side his mouth, while the other one is still on the ground pretending to be badly hurt.

G.K. with a cold stare, allows him to come close.

The mysterious gallant knight, assuming a fighting karate stand, clinching his fists, comes to a fighting distance. Before he takes any action talks to G.K:

"Let's see if you can manage to fight me as you did with the other two, I am a black belt in Karate…" and with out any warning he turns his body right ways -180 degrees- and by pivoting left ways on his left leg, executes a back kick, aiming at G.K's abdomen. The kick is well executed but as soon as the leg is stretched to find its target, he screams with pain and holds his foot that just kicked, while falling on the ground.

That happens because G.K. anticipated the kick and moves his body slightly back, avoiding it. He then springs forward as fast as he avoided the kick, and by executing a front kick with his right rear leg, kicking his opponent under his stretched leg, behind his knee.

G.K. warns him as he tries to lift himself up.

"Don't try to get up. Your leg will be num for about an hour."

G.K. continues to talk to him in a very calm manner:

"A really Karate - ka which you claim to be, would never look for that kind of fake Gallantry by getting involved with people like him" (G.K. points at the man on the ground where he is already getting up and staring at the girl, where she is also staring at him with surprise).

"Your Karate Teacher must told you of not to use your knowledge in a bad light. For the shake of Karate, you deserve worse punishment than that…"

G.K. noticed the pretender of been hit to try to run a way.

He quickly puts his right hand in side his left side pocket of his jacket and pulls out a dart with a steel front and throws it with not much speed and power, towards the runaway's shaft place of his backside. The dart finds its target making the man stop and screaming, trying to reach the dart with his right hand.

G.K. beckons him to come to him while he walks towards the thug.

He grabs him from his ear like a bad little boy and pulls the dart out of his behind, directs him towards the girl where she is still dusting herself off, while she is looking in surprise at the well-dressed man.

His condition is very bad and funny as he tries hard not to scream from the pain of the dart and his cloths are torn in some places with his face dirty from the ground.

As they approached the girl, G.K. noticed that apart of her well-trimmed body she has a beautiful face as well.

While he asks her to tell him the reason of why they were pulling her like that, their eyes met that close for a first time.

The girl looks at him very carefully, tries to study him, not much as he is attractive or not, but as for his culpabilities. Eventually, not only she does not introducing herself, but in some ways commands him to leave the mans ear as he is not involved with the others (Referring the two unconscious men) and tells him:

"He is also a victim!"

G.K. without leaving the man's ear, tells her politely that he will:

"Providing you will tell me of what happened first. Please tell me everything, I am not a Policeman but something tells me that you are in a peculiar situation and the outcome will surprise you!"

The girl looks at him strait in his eyes, analyzing him again; she takes a deep breath and tells him her story:"I came here with my car. Akis was with me," (She points at the man where G.K holds him by his ear). She continuous by saying:

"When we came out of the car, these three men attacked us with out a reason. They came out of the bushes like they were waiting for us."

G.K., while she talks, cannot help admiring her beautiful blue eyes.

"I can only understand that they wanted to kidnap me for 400,000 euro, as they told me earlier."

G.K. shaking his head, and after some thinking asks her:

"Whose idea was to come to Olympus?" Although he was afraid he new the answer!

While she looks surprised to his question, she tells him that the idea was: "Akis."As the girl finishes her last word, which was… Akis; she opens her beautiful eyes in surprise when she sees G.K. striking her friend on his face with his right open palm, sending him to find the other two, where are sleeping on the ground, with the fourth one useless to help them.

To the girls complain, G.K. assures her that Aki was involved and he masterminded the whole idea. He tells her that they should inform the Police.

The girl tells him that she rather calls her Father from the secret telephone fitted in the car, but asks him politely not to follow her.

Now, it was his time to get surprised, but never the less he agrees with her and he walks to his motorcar.

He opens the driver's door to take the net and place in the boot (Trunk), but on top of the ruin net he finds something like a very large… diamond, with the size of a large egg.

He takes it in his palm and he examines it. It is really a diamond.

He looks up, and although there were no clouds, he saw a lightning across the sky, following it by a thunder.With his eyes towards the sky G.K. talks with respect and excitement:

"Thank you Athena! Thank you!"

While his eyes are looking up thanking the Goddess; he does not noticed two beautiful blue eyes where are not only looking in surprised at the sky, but also looking with more surprised at the man who just saved her:

"Now… he is talking to the thunders and lightning." The girl said talking to somebody on a cordless phone…

## CHAPTER FOUR
### 2 hours later

In the lounge of an expensive villa on the outskirts of Athens, two men are seating on comfortable armchairs. The one is G.K. and the other is a Special International Government Secret Employee (IGSE) for Law and Order on World Scale, under the umbrella of United Nations, age about 60-65 years old.

The IGSE is breaking the silence: "Your story is unbelievable, could you tell me how you came back to Greece after 21 years and where were you all this time? Do you have any relatives? Are you married? What is your full name?"

G.K. answers to the IGSE very calmly, but his voice has something like he is commanding not explaining or apologizing:

"It is unnecessary to tell you everything now, but I am clearly convinced that all was organized by Goddess Athena! The fact that I was there at the Mt. Olympus where at the same time your daughter needed help and that you are a Government Secret Employee for Law and Order; you could assist me with documents and a position to the Secret Organization, which as you are telling me it is sponsored by the United Nations, where includes the United States of America, so I can carry out my pledge to Goddess Athena and assist our country and the World, to fight crime as it manifests."

"Goddess Athena, Goddess Athena, who is going to believe all these" ask the IGSE.

G.K. with the speed of lightning gets up from the armchair, takes out the diamond from his pocket and placed it on the coffee table next to IGSE.

"This diamond I founded inside my car on the Mountain while your daughter was phoning you."

The IGSE takes the diamond in his hand. He gets up and walks out of the large lounge, coming back with a magnified glass and starts examine the stone. While he examines it, he talks to himself.

"How on hell this stone came into my hands, where I am the most expert in this Country for valuing this kind of germ?" By saying that he turns to G.K. and tells him:

"This diamond represents a tremendous amount of money, could be over a billion Euro. I ought to have you arrested as…"

Suddenly a bright light comes from no where falls upon the IGSE and the voice of Goddess Athena sounds like a thunder in the quiet lounge as she appears in a form of a shadow.

"Your name is P.N… Your secret number is A5" (Athens 5). "You have served as an IGSE for 12 years. You have made a pledge to our Country until you die to fight crime at all costs. You employ and dismiss your Agents who are of the elite of the Greek Rule. Your job is to stop the bad elements at your choosing. Our Country and the World owes you a lot. I selected you to take G.K. under your wings. My small present to him is for all his human endurance that went through the tests for 21 years by the Spirits of 11 Ancient Olympic Champions and a living Greek - South African Master, whose name is very familiar to you. The living Master is George Karavidas; where apart of his amazing skills he is well educated and helps secretly the Organization that you are a distinguish member. The Master will train G.K. for the rest of his life, as he will make him his successor… Take the diamond, valuated and legally bank the money in his name. He will tell you his Identity, but you will give him another, as A6 (Athens 6). You will register him at the Unites Nations."

The Goddess penetrates the eyes of the IGSE as she carries on:

"Allocate some houses in the most major Cities all over the world, as he will fight crime internationally. Although he will take orders only from you, but after they (The FBI, the CIA, and INTERPOL etc.) will find out about his amazing record, they will possibly use him for difficult and dangerous tasks? Very soon he will be based in Boston USA, not by anybody's order, but by himself. You must not hesitate to let him go to Boston, as he knows how to handle all situations! Although he is very experience with all modern guns and explosives of all kinds, he will never kill! I will reappear again to your successor, but I guarantee to you of many - many more years of active life, as our Country needs you alive, and with many more years of retirement with your family. Soon you must leave for the United States, to go and fetch your wife from the Hospital, as she is recuperating rapidly and now she is walking again."

The Goddess softens her voice as she speaks to G.K.

"I will always be near you, and when you need me, you only have to call me or think of me, but I will appear if I chose too! You do that only when is necessary! Good luck to both of you!"

The light comes off and the Goddess disappears.


CHAPTER FIVE


April 2006, although appears to say goodbye, in a manner of been kind with the temperature of going over than 25 Celsius, all of a sudden the weather bureau warns the Athenians to be prepared for heavy rains, accompanied by winds for most of the Country, with the temperature going down between 12 to 16 Celsius…

The rain has started in Athens just before 6 p.m. and continued until 8 p.m.

Only, during these two hours of heavy rain, it was enough to make most of the roads in and around Athens to be flooded, thus, making it difficult to the motorists to move around…

Just as well, this night, while his new friends went to USA for a weak, G.K. decided to go to the movies, to see `Alexander the Great` who was just released at the `Cinemax Complex`, The Cinema was at Marousi (A north Suburb of Athens), which was only two kilometers away from his home.

Although he had difficulty to find parking, eventually he parked his car near

the subway station, and walked the 200 meters, taking his time, as it was only 8:15 p.m.

On his way to the Cinema, he noticed a bright sign on the topside of the complex, which tingle his interests as it reminded him of Port Elizabeth…

The sign was written: `Ten Pin Bowling`…

In South Africa, at his free time, G.K. apart of going hunting and playing Tennis, frequently visited with some Rival - Friends the Ten Pin Bowling Alley. It was a time of relaxing his body of the vigorous exercises, but energizing his mind as he enjoyed the concentration of how to strike the pins…

As he had time until 9 o clock where the main picture would start; he decided to go and watch…

As he entered the Alley, he observed with satisfaction that families and friends were playing together making fun of it, teasing each other when the ball went out of its `way` entering the gutter, missing the `Plastic Bottles`.

He noticed some tables with comfortable armchairs.

He sat down, ordering an orange juice to the blond girl waitress, who looked at him with more interests as one waiter looks to a newcomer customer.

Although casual, he looked well dressed with classical gray pants, gray shirt with a dark blue tie, covering his well - trained body by a dark - blue double breasted with golden buttons blazer. As for his shoes, were black leather boots, Italian made...

The blond waitress brought him the Juice.

After paid the girl, he lifted the glass to taste the juice... That time he felt some body looking at him.

He turned to his right and saw, not one but two pair of eyes trying to attract his attention.

The distance was about 3 meters away from his table, and clearly he could see the one pair of eyes was blue color, with the second pair appearing to be green.

The green eyes were belonging to a beautiful brunet, with chestnut long hair. Her body was well trained but needed more exercise as its owner looked like she had a tendency to eat more sweets than usual.

As for the blue eyes, her owner was a blond beauty, with her hair also long. Her body was well trim, reminding of an International Fashion girl at its best.

Both girls could be between the ages of 20 to 22 years old.

When the dark brown Mediterranean eyes of George, met with the Anglo-Saxon's green and blue eyes of the girls, then...they both bow to him with respect!

This kind of respect, regardless the color of the eyes, it could only be learned inside the Dojo (Gym) of a Karate club, or at any Karate tournament, in and out of the fighting area.

G.K., not to be rood (Because he didn't recognized the girls yet), he gets up and also bows to them. While he was looking, trying to see and fill that something who will help him recognize them, he thought that they could be from South Africa, as they both appeared to be more English or Scandinavians - like, than Greek.

With out hesitation, he nods them to come to his table.

Both the girls agreed, looking very happy for the invitation.

As they turned to talk to the three other girls who were together, explaining the reason of why they had to leave them, G.K. by looking at them, tried to `read` of what they were saying, as one of his special qualities was, to `Read Lips`. By `reading their lips, he realized that he was right about them as they were explaining in Greek to their friends, that they new him from South Africa.

As the blue eyed who was doing all the talking to her friends, turned her back by doing a natural karate movement, then... G.K. remembered both of them; taking part in 2002 Nationals...They both took part at the National all styles Karate c/ships, at the university of Pretoria (Pretoria is the Capital of South Africa), where G.K. took part as George Karavidas Junior, winning 3 gold medals:

Please Note:
The first medal, was for Kumite (Free fight), for under 65 kilograms, where to reach the final, he needed to win 7 times, as the 8th was for a gold medal, which means, if Karate was an Olympic sport, the winning fights for a gold, could be less!

The second gold medal was for Kata (Formal Exercise), where G.K. did his style Kata, which was creation of Master George Karavidas. Again he had to take part in two groups of 32 participants in each group, which means to reach the finals; he had to win at least 6 times.

The third was the most difficult, as it was the Open Kumite, where only the first, second and third winners of every division could take part, which means, fighters from under -60 -65 -70 kilograms etc. up and included over 85 Kilograms as well, could take part.

These two girls, where were now are greeting him by shaking hands and bowing, they took part in a Team Kata and Team Kumite, with G.K. as a Chief Referee (Floor Controller) on both categories.

The girls took 2nd place on both categories against the teams of 16 provinces.

G.K.'s girl's team won the first place for Kata and Kumite.

Please also note: The team Kata, consists of three Athletes – Karate - ka where one is placed in the center and in front, with the other two behind him/her at the left and right, thus, forming a triangle with the one in front.

The Kata has to be performed like one person, synchronized all the moves, like Athletes Team when doing floor exercises, only, Karate is more difficult because it has to have: Perfect balance, co ordination, power, focus, harmony, speed, target, even synchronized breathing.

It's absolutely ecstatic to watch Team Kata, but must be performed by advanced Karate-ka, where they have practiced together regular for more than three years. As for the Karate-ka himself/herself who takes part in the c/ships, either individual or as a team, at the time of performance of two and a half to three minutes, he/she is in another World...

As for the Kumite (Fight), we will analyze it later on!

They all seated and the conversation started, first in English, with some Greek words in between, and with G.K. calling the waiter to offer them juices.

"Girls, when they called your names over the Microphone, your surname sounded like you were English, and when I first saw you earlier looking at me, I thought it as well, but now that you are more closed, I could sworn that one, or both of your parents could be Greek.

"Sensei (Karate Teacher), in some ways you are not far from correct," said the one with the blond hair, who had introduced herself as Joan.
"My Greek name is Joanna (I-o-anna) and my Mother is Greek, born here in Marousi. When my Mother at her last year of her studies at the University of Cape Town as a Pediatrician, met with my Father from London, who was in Cape Town for his Masters Degree, also for Pediatric. They fall in love at first sight. In six months time they got married, and strait away they were transferred to Pretoria, where the Government appointed my Father to be in charge of the New Pediatric Hospital, just on the outskirts of the Capital – City. So, although my Father is English, born in London, his Mother was born also in London from Greek Parents. That's why my surname is Johnson, because my Granny `took` her surname of her English Husband, who incidentally his Mother was also Greek... To make it more complicated for you, I will tell you that my Johnson Grandparents, are came back to leave here, honoring their Greek

Ancestors…They must of have visiting Parthenon over 50 times and have going to Olympia and all the Ancient sites, including the Islands, just as many; setting an example to us all, for not forgetting our inheritance! Concluding my story, I will add that:I used to come here every summer from South Africa, but the last two years I study at the National Academy and I am going to South Africa for Christmas and Easter time. As for June - July - August, I stay here, because in South Africa is winter, but my Parents are coming here, and we visit few Islands, including Myconos of course. That's all about me! My friend will talk for herself."

"Something like that is my story as well," said the girl call Mary (Mary in Greek, comes from Maria).

"I was born in Cyprus from a Greek Mother born in South Africa and from Greek Father where were born and bread in Cyprus. Now, my surname sounds as Michael, but in Greek is…"

"Me-cha-el", the three said it together, laughing.

"I also study at the National Academy," Mary continues:

"I stay in Kastri, (Kastri, is a suburb between Marousi and Dionysus, where G.K. stays) with my Aunt, Sister of my Father."

"Now Sensei that you have learned about us," said Joan. "What would you say if you tell us little about your self? Starting with couple of questions from both of us? Like…what happened, and why you are in Greece? Are you going to open a club for your style? As your Greek Nationality is well known, not only by all the female Black Belts of South Africa, but also by the male Black Belts, who had the bad luck to Kumite (Fight) with you! As for your Kata…you never had any really opponent, except one or two from your own style, the

Shotokounthigh – Pagratio, who's Creator is Master George Karavidas, your Father!"

Until the time where the young girl so naturally mentioned that his Master was his Father, from then on, his own heart started doing Kumite with the Reality:

"Joan, you surprised me, by knowing so much about my Style and myself. As for my Master, who never calls his Creation, a `Style` but `Art of Fighting`, I regret to inform you that he is not… my Father."

"Really," both shouted, almost scream.

"But you do not only have the same surname, you also have the same name, calling you Junior… You are Greek, aren't you?" Said Joan, opening her adorable mouth and blue eyes to the limits, thus making G.K. feeling uncomfortable.

Although Joan had surprise G.K., she didn't surprised Mary, because when they were looking at G.K. earlier, it was Joan who said to Mary after grabbing her from her arm:

"Do you believe in destiny? Finally I will meet him after all!"

At the other side of the table, where G.K. was seated; after took a deep breath, he answers to the blond beauty:

"Yes, I am Greek! I was born in Piraeus (The main Port of Greece), from Greek parents of course." (According to the documents where were in the Orphanage, he was telling them the truth, but he didn't know for sure, because he couldn't even remembered his Parents, never mind the place he was born).

"From a young age, I lost my Parents and I immigrated to South Africa, staying with some relatives. It was then when I met the Master who took care of me while I learned his Art, as he hasn't got any children of his own. I am a Qualified Athleatiatros (Athletes -

Doctor) and a Psychologist. Further more, I have interests in Physics and Electronics. But these and other Sciences or anything else, are coming second to my only love, which is the Shotokounthigh Art of Fighting, who has its roots back in the Ancient Era of Pagratio..."

"We know everything about it!" Said Mary where this time she is coming first, beating Joan to the second...

Not to be out - smart, Joan directed the conversation to her way:

"You said everything else is coming second?" She asks with a meaning.

"What about feelings, love for a woman, Sex?"

G.K. understood her meaning all the way. Things could be different if he was alone with her; but he was going to give her a lesson anyway, giving the moderate Mary some satisfaction too.

He gets closer to her face, looking deep into her magnificent blue eyes and without blinking, he is telling her:

"Joanna! For now, I will tell you this: Whatever comes, let it come, as I do not only encourage it, but some times like tonight, by calling both of you to come to me, I started it as well. With one condition though... no Commitment! I will tell you also that my blood is all the way Mediterranean and with the combination of a clean life and body exercise..."

Joan, interrupts him by grabbing his right wrist and comes more closed to his face, almost toughing his lips with hers.

"You mean that you are... very, very, Hot?"

"Joanna!" Said Mary quickly with a dose of jealousy: "You are going to - far..."

"I will answer! Please Mary," said G.K. smiling, and while he was saying that to her, comes closed toughing her chick, then rubbed her neck, making Joan ready to burst...

He leans back to his comfortable armchair, telling Joan:

"When you were looking at me few minutes ago, it was the same way when you were looked at my direction in South Africa in 2002...I have to admitted though; when I didn't see you taking part in the following year..."

"You mean you were thinking of me the whole year?" asks Joan grabbing his arm again getting closer to his face ready to kiss him.

"Yes, I was thinking of you, but on one hand I didn't have the time to look for you, and one the other, I was dating out another girl from Scotland."

"Which you don't date her anymore!" Said Joan not only persisting but takes his right hand and kissed it, then... kissing his lips as well, holding his head with both her hands.

G.K. touches her chick, but not like he did with Mary, and slowly retracts his hand and his face, apologizing... to Mary, while answering to Joan:

"No Joan, my affair with the Scottish girl is still on, but as I told you earlier, `no commitment`. Please don't interrupt me, let me finish. Her name is Janet and we have a relationship, like I have with other girls, but this particular one, I see her more often, because she teaches my Art at one of our Dojo's in South Africa. But also, even where I was at my teens I never liked kiss or being kissed in public. Actually I had very little time in between to my school studies and to five - hour practice, save only to some weekends..."

"So, that's why you apologized to me earlier." Said Mary:

"Not only for that, but to ask you as well... and if you like the three of us to become friends, at least as long as I am in Greece, either the three of us together or separate, but with out commitment. If you both like the idea I'll go and buy another two tickets for Matrix.

CHAPTER SIX

With the weather becoming worse, and with wins of more than 9 Boffor (About 60 miles an hour), accompanied by heavy rain, G.K.'s company
  agreed in the end, to go with him to the cinema, also Agreed to visit his friend's Restaurant.

Now, they are all seated inside G.K.'s white BMW, driving for the Restaurant.

Joan earlier moved quickly to seat next to G.K., leaving Mary to be alone in the back seat.
  Although Mary should be the one to complain, in the end Joan was grinning with jealousy, because Mary was leaning forward to talk and be into the conversation about the movie, she was getting very closed to G.K.'s face, even breathing on his neck and inhaling his Old Spice...
  They entered Irene road, which was the extension of Pericleous street, with G.K. have the windscreen wipers in full speed, driving very carefully. They took a 90 - degree left turn over the bridge, entering the High Way with out any traffic at all.
  They carried on for about 10 minutes when they saw the sign to Peristeri (Pigeon – City). G.K. soon realized that the roads were flooded and some of them were under construction, leaving some back streets free, but again with a lot of water. He took a left turn hopefully to get to

the right road, but because he never visited the Restaurant from that direction, possible he took a wrong turn.

"Girls, I think we are lost," said jokingly, "but lets take that road to the right and if it is not flooded we will be there in few minutes."

As soon as he turned to the right he said:

"Oh! It looks like its O.K., no floods… but… there is something over there, oh Hell, somebody with a motorbike…he must of have an accident on the Cross - Road? Could be hit and run? The bike looks like is on top of his leg…something is not right!"

He stops the car about 4 meters away, flicking the lights. The fallen man lifts his left arm, appeals for help in Greek…

G.K. tells the girls not to come out, but they must be alert. He switches the engine off and removes the keys, through them in to his pocket, leaving the Head Lights on.

It still raining but not much as he gets out of the car, but instead of going to the injured man, he circles around his car, moving like a cat. He senses danger again. He looks around, but sees nobody. He is now at Mary's window and as soon as he passes the co drivers door, ignoring the open blue eyes of Joan; suddenly stops next to the right fender as he felt a cold wind from his right side.

He turned his head sharp to the right and first felt, then saw, a man wearing a balaclava covering his face, and with his right head swinging a black Baseball Butt, to strike his right knee, possible both his knees.

But G.K.'s knees weren't there… He touches the bonnet of his car with his left hand, lifting both knees towards his chest, thus the Butt strikes `fresh air`.

The thug swears at himself as he retracts the Butt, and swings it, aiming this time the head of G.K.

This dark unpleasant – moody night, where those two thugs were waiting for their prey to fall into their trap, where they thought had set it so professionally, to earn some easy money, appeared that they luck wasn't only running out, but went against them, as their prey, turned out to be their worst deadly enemy and tonight would be their last time of harming innocent people…

The second strike was much harder than the first one, but this time the Greek Junior Master wasn't only ready and waiting for him, but he had the time to insult himself, for not kicking his assailant while he was on the air.

As the Butt comes furiously to strike his head from the side, which could be G.K.'s left ear, didn't find its target because he blocks it with his left arm. If the block wasn't properly executed, then, the arm most probably would be broken, damaging his ear - drum as well!

But these movements of blocking from all directions, to cover all parts of the body, with many and deferent instruments and weapons, from all the` sizes` of the assailants, G.K. had done them over a million times each defense! So much during the ten year period with the Spirits of the Ancient Olympic Winners and so much and more with the Greek Living Master in South Africa as well.

The` more`, were in the last Ten endless years, where the Master taught his student, for every defend, to retaliate almost simultaneously…

This is what the loyal and worthy student did, like he did it in practice, but saved his life and possible saved the lives of the two innocent girls as well…

Straight after the block, he retaliated by doing the fastest movement towards the assailant, by punching him to his face with his right fist, breaking his two front upper teeth and two of the bottom, as the punch was vertical, covering both parts of his mouth. The punch not only broke his teeth but shattered his dreams also, who instead of going on vacation for stealing a new BMW and reaping the valuables of all three humans in it...he will go now not only to the Dentist, but to the Gnatho - Specialist (Jaw - Bone Doctor) as his jaw was fractured as well. And that wasn't all, because as soon as G.K. punched him to the jaw, he followed by a slide sidekick to solar plexus as well, breaking some ribs and sending him doing somersaults backwards...

When G.K. turned to see the other thug, he heard Joanna and Mary worn him, while at the same time they opened their doors.

The `fallen` one, where in fact was the bait, wasn't wounded after all!

He lifts himself up as he was on top of the bike, with the greatest of ease. His mistake was (As always they do) that he wasted few valuable seconds to study his bike and to pull down his cap, to cover his face, making it a balaclava... It was then, when G.K. senses danger again...

He takes a large step with his left foot towards the `Bait. He then pivots on it left ways, when at the same time he lifts his right leg above of the bike, executes a round house kick to the side and back of his body, shattering not only his ribs but damaging permanently the thugs right kidney as well!

The kick was executed with a snap, which means the leg retracted in a manner that was ready to kick again and not get mixed up when the cyclist while falling down with his bike, taken the same position as before on the road, only this time he was forced to do it from the opposite side, which means that the left foot landed under the bike (not the right as it was before)…While falling with his bike on top of his left leg, he tried to stop the fall by placing his palm on the road, only to fracture his wrist and broke his thumb.

G.K. didn't pay much attention of his condition, because he heard a metallic noise striking the wet road…

With out any surprise, he sees a gun with a silencer on it.

He jumps over the thug and takes it in to his hands. It looked like a Berretta 9mm.

G.K. turns the gun to the Assailant with the Baseball Butt, who is getting up swearing at his accomplish, spitting out some of his teeth, holding his stomach with the left hand and still…holding the Butt with his right. The distance is about 5 meters.

When the thug sees the gun, he turns around and… he is still running, with the Butt on his right hand.

At this time, a car comes from behind, with the driver flicking his lights to pass.

"I think I saved his life," said G. K. talking to himself.

After looking at the man on the bike, he walks towards the car, hiding the gun behind him to tell the man of what happened…but the driver comes out of the car still holding the door open. He sees a Gentleman, who looks like he is going to a party, but…he hides something behind his back. Without any hesitation, he gets into his car again, hits the reveres gear and at the first corner, disappears.

"Sensei, he is leaving!" Mary shouted at G.K.

He turns and while he walks back, he observes pathetic scenery, with the actor and director the thug who earlier was playing innocent victim of an accident…

While limping trying to run away, by holding and running his bike with him, which it refuses to start at his kicks. Eventually when he stops swearing at it, then it starts.

With a great effort he mounts the bike and accelerates a way, with out looking back.

"Let him go!" He says while he examines the gun thoroughly.

Although his Master taught him a lot about guns with hundreds of target shooting from deferent positions and conditions of the weather; concentrated mostly of how to disarm them, using as a helping tool, apart of different weapons, also his arms and legs as well. On the other hand, taught G.K. to despise guns, as he values the human's life more that anything else. Actually he used to tell him a proverb of his own:

"The Humans Life is very short anyway, why we must make it shorter?"

G.K. tells the girls to come in the car.

He starts the engine telling them that he has to do something first before going to the Restaurant:

"Oh! The rain finally stops." Mary said just to make a conversation,

"What a night?" Said Joan.

G.K. while listening to the girls, he unscrews the silencer and taking out the bullets one by one. He then stops at the first corner and with the engine running he gets out of the car. He walks to the sewerage and throws them inside, including the magazine. He then drives to the next corner and stops again. Then, in front of the eyes of the astonished girls, and with a help of small screwdriver that took from the side pocket of his cars door, dismantles the gun in two pieces. He takes the one piece and gets out again throwing it in the sewerage.

He stopped once more for the last piece.

The time, the weather and the date, were in favor of this kind of delivery to the sewerages, with out taking a risk to be seen by any passing car.

"I should keep one bullet as a souvenir, but the sooner I forget this incident the better, because I could never imagine that things like that happened in my Country. I still can't believe it!"

The two well trained girls although appeared to be calm, they weren't, because in side the Dojo (Gym), they were learning to take part in the competition Karate, where injuring your opponent will loose points. The part of self – defense, although doing it with an opponent and most of the techniques were some how realistic, but again, the raw street fight is completely deferent...so, tonight where they had the experience at first - hand, will not only be unforgettable, but at the first change they will definitely seat down and talk to each other of changing styles!

G.K. who understood their mixed feelings said to them in a friendly manner:

"Girls, in few minutes we will be at the Restaurant, do not hesitate to ask me any questions..."

## CHAPTER SEVEN
### At the Restaurant


G.K. introduced the girls to the family.

To start with, they ordered a Sea - Food Platter for four people and green salad.

Although none of them liked alcohol, they all decided to taste the traditional ouzo (With water of course), for not betray the tradition way of their Forefathers!

`Ouzo is colorless and tastes like tequila" (So they say).


"The first and the last ouzo I ever tasted, was about 8 years ago in South Africa, at the Birthday Party of one of my Greek colleagues at the University of Port Elizabeth, who brought it with him from Mytilini (An Island of Greece)," G.K. said.


"I haven't tasted yet!" Said Joan, "but Mary and I, we have tried some Scots Whisky, also in South Africa."

"How about you Mary?" said G.K. smiling, "did you Sin, by trying ouzo?"

"Oh yes! We have tasted many times in my home in Cyprus, with my younger brother. We always have it at home. Actually my grandfather is using it for medicine as well. But one thing is for sure; ouzo tastes much better than whisky!" They all laughed.


At this relaxing time, it was when G.K. rested his elbows on the table, and Mary, who was looking at him while she was talking about ouzo, noticed that he grimacing with pain.

"What is wrong Sensei?" She asks him, in a Motherhood manner, ready to attend his wounds (Any wounds), especially in front of Joanna.

G.K. with out answering, he removes his jacket and hangs it on top of his chair, nodding and tell to his friend Mr. Dimitri, the proprietor of the Restaurant, to bring him a coca cola bottle, but he mustn't open it! He then, unbuttons his left sleeve and lift's it up, unveiling the injury that happened from the blocking of the Base Ball Butt. It was slightly swollen up, with some blood - stains on it...

This time was when the always - pleasant Dimitri, is bringing the coca cola and sees the injury that G.K. unsuccessfully tried to hide it from him.He gets sad, even when G.K. tells him that it's nothing:
"Accidentally in the Gym, this is what happened when somebody is careless" said G.K. blaming himself, but smiling. "It will be O.K..."
"You accidentally, it's hard to believe it!"
He leaves the bottle on the table and carries on:
"The little I know of you; the only person, who can harm you, is... only yourself... If you need some ice, then call me!"

When Dimitri walks away satisfied of his philosophy, which didn't touch G.K., but touched and satisfied the two girls where they exchanged glances, shacking their heads left right, meaning that at last they find the right person to practice their Karate with, and learn something useful and effective.
G.K. although observed everything, he pretend the opposite. He turns the bottle flat on the table and places his sore arm on it, rolling in it up and down, pressing it more on the wounded part... He kept doing it for about five minutes, thus, taking the benefit out of the ice to let the pain subside and the swelling getting down.
While keeping the arm on to the bottle, to ease the atmosphere, G.K. asks the girls of a technical question:

"Girls, Question? The single upper block (Age uke), which I did it against the Butt, why I escaped with this minor injury and I didn't break my arm, although I have blocked thousands of times this kind of attack, with more dangerous weapons, such as, broken bottles, knives, spears, and police globs with fitted knives in them, even irons? Does it sound logical in theory that my arm should be broken, as I went and blocked `against the force` of the Butt? Will you give me an answer?"

Looking at their faces, he realizes that the girls were developing questions to the question asks, G.K had not difficulty of realizing the commercial way or the ignorance of the person who taught these two and so many other girls and boys, with out giving them the proper explanation...

"Ladies, because of the time limit in the Dojo, your Instructor never had the change explaining to you in detail about every technique, but, he should of doing it much earlier, at the beginner's classes. That time is where he - the Instructor- `enters` the student in to the Art. At the later stage, again the Instructor `develops` the student with theoretical and practical applications, non - stop, insisting in detail! The Teaching - Instructor, to be able to develop and then pass his knowledge, has to be very closed and for many - many years to the Master himself, or at least, with the highest in Rank if the Creator is not alive...Anyway, now that we have the change, I will explain to you -in theory-, the incident that we all experienced, but before that, let me attack with my fork this large and juicy prone, which I suggest that you doing the same as me, because very soon you will not find anything to fight on the platter...

Not to be outsmart, the two fighting girls, started attacking the sea - food platter, by using their forks to cutch their pray, their fingers to do the anatomy and by using their health teeth to eliminate the unlucky Prone. But they didn't stop there; systematically and with a great speed, attacked and stripped from their shells the Lobsters and five other different kinds of fish, making G.K. laughing, but open his eyes as well:

<With a proper instruction, they will be very effective fighters! > He thought smiling.

While he was awaiting his change to enter the fight...he calls his friend:

"Dimitri, we will stay on this menu! Please make and bring another two sea - food platters with another two green salads, but no more ouzo! You can bring us a large bottle of spring water instead. Thanks Dimitri that will be all!"

While walking away to the kitchen, the kind shop – keeper asked G.K.:

"Do you want me to bring you some bread, heated on the barbeque grill with Mrs. Soula's (His wife) special sauce?"

G.K. quickly asked the already busy girls, about his friend's gesture... After their answered, he lifted his thump up, indicating O.K.

After few minutes

"Sensei, I have a Question" Said Mary, carried on:

"I observed that, after the slide sidekick (Yoko Geri - Sabaki) to the one with the Butt, you didn't retract your leg, but with your Round House Kick (Mawashi Geri) to the one with the gun, you returned it!"

"Exactly!" said Joan, embracing Mary...

"Very good observation by both of you, but before I analyze them I have to go back a bit, to why and where we must or we mustn't retract our foot, or our arm, for that matter."

G.K. looks at both the girls deep into their eyes to see if its worth the effort to help them, but to his satisfaction, they both were waiting very anxiously to learn, as they didn't have enough information in the past...

"As you know, my Art its not Japanese, but, because we compete against all Japanese Karate Arts, thus, we use the same rules and regulations as far as the competition is concern, but when it comes to the street fight, or better say to `survival` when ones life is in danger, then the Philosophy depends heavily on the Creator of the Art. Lucky for me I am very closed to Master George Karavidas..."

Both girls observed that this man of steel, just by only mentioned his Masters name, he becomes emotional...

"But" he carries on. "Although most of the people involved in Martial Arts, thinking that I am his Son; he does the same with all of his Instructor-Students. He doesn't only pay attention to the very little detail, but he explains it thoroughly. You know why? Because whatever he creates, before he puts it into action, he has done it hundreds of times from all angles, with or with out opponent, in and out of the Dojo, in the sand, on top of rocks, even inside the water! Also, many times he carries a baby doll in his arm, fighting with the rest of the other parts of his body ...The reason for that is his desire to help a Mother or a Father who are holding their child in their arms and had been attacked...

"Unbelievable" said Joan.

"Oh my God!" said Mary, making the sign of cross, while carries on: "If I haven't see of what you were capable of doing, I could say that of what you are telling us is far fetched, and you have a lot of imagination. But now, I will definitely meet your Shihan, which although uses the Japanese rules in his Rank, as well as the competition rules, he applies his own Way and Philosophy, where their roots derives direct from our Greek Ancestors. You are very lucky indeed to leave with him!"

"Question?" said Joan, who has difficulty calling him Sensei. "Although everything went so fast, I had a change to see when you block to the Butt; your palm was open, not closed, as we have learned it in our style. Does it make any difference and why?"

"Joan, you are coming to my question where I asked you both earlier. Don't be surprise if I tell you that I saw your eyes watching the action while I blocked the Butt; but lets go back to the mechanism of the trap, shall we? Do you want me to explain it to you in detail?"

"Yes! Yes!" They both said, while stop eating…

He looks again to their beautiful eyes and he couldn't help asking himself of which one of the two would he prefer to be more intimated…he concluded that up to now the odds were even…

"Now listen and look carefully! The strike with the Butt wasn't direct downwards but at about at 45 degrees angle towards my head, thus, if I didn't have to block it I could be hit on my left ear or at the side of my temple, possibly on the neck as well. Very dangerous…could be death, if it had been connected to one of the three I just mentioned. But inside of this dangerous time of my life -

and yours- I had one advantage… that was as from the time the Butt was lifted until the time of connection, I had more than one second to convert my block to my advantage with a limited of injury, by using his speed and power against him!"

G.K. stops Mary's question by lifting his palm and carries on:

"But I didn't have the space, thus, I blocked the Butt's speed by intercepting it. Here again the practical experience counted in my favor, which means that the glob (Lets call it glob) instead to land on my arm at eighty miles an hour, it landed only at thirty miles, because I went against the speed of it, thus, I moved my arm forward to block it, reducing the speed… Now! One could get injured still, but by using the correct angle of my arm, with the open palm, bending the thump as well…like this! G.K. saws them the block, as at this hour there were nobody else in the Restaurant.

"So! First, by using the right angle of my arm, made the glob to slide slightly, and second, by open the palm and bending the thump, I energized to the limits the tendons and the muscles around the elbow bones. Thus, the swelling comes from the muscles and tendons only, which means tomorrow I will be O.K… I may have though to use some ice tonight at my home as well…"

"Now!" G.K. carries on. "Before I will explain to you further; there few simple reasons in competition of returning the leg:

First, when you are kicking your opponent (Almost in all kinds of kicks to the body) and you do not want to be caught (Grabbed) by the opponent's hand, then, after your kick, you bring your leg back.

Second, also, if possible, you do not want to give him a change to block your attack (Usually by his hand). Thus, on both cases, you do not give your opponent a change to retaliate effectively..."

The junior but experience Sensei asks the girls if they understood him up to this point.

"Yes! Yes! They both said, like they were twins, when one anticipates the other.

"As for scoring is concern, when you do not pull your leg back, and you connect to opponents body, then, by rules, it consider of `no scoring` as the kick is `pushed` and out of control. Even could be a foul. But you know that, don't you?"

"Yes" Yes". They both agreed again.

"On the Front Kick though", G.K. carries on, "I will tell you another reason of bringing the leg back, either in Competition or in the Street: In your effort to connect effectively to your opponent's body, usually you stretch your hip forward, but if you miss him and you strike `air`, then you can loose balance and fall..."

He stops the explanation, as the food is getting cold!

"Girls...the rest for the front and other kicks, I will explain them to you in the Dojo, or some other time!"

"Please Sensei! You promised to tell us about the `trap`?" asks Mary, with the approval of Joan.

"Yes I will! But lets first re - attack the Sea - Food, because my friend is bringing the two platters and they appeared to be very heavy for him."

As Dimitri approaches, G.K. lifts the almost empty tray and placed it on top of the next table, making space for the fresh ones.

"We stopped at the punch to his teeth," said Joan, after Dimitry left.

"You said it with so much satisfaction, like you herself were the one who did the defense". Said Mary laughing.

"O.K.! After the `vertical` punch to his face, then I followed up by a slide side kick with the right leg to his flabby stomach, and felt that I damaged some of his ribs as well, but at the time of the impact; first I felt, then I heard metal scratching behind me, thus, quickly I `dropped` the kicking leg on the ground (Not retracted) and when I turned, I realized that I had only four seconds before he dismounts his bike and possible he could shoot me... So, I balanced myself by bending the right kicking leg, thus, I created a spring to my other leg. Then, I took a large step forward as you both saw, and kicked him with the right leg to his ribs. If you noticed, I connected to his ribcage with the ball of my foot and not with the instep! Which means the shoe made the impact more painful... and definitely two or three ribs broke instantly, and as the time pass then the pain will be unbearable, but by not bringing back the right leg earlier, I gain almost two valuable seconds..."

"Sensei, why you let them go?" asks Mary.
"The reason is very simple: Those two thugs, after the lesson they learned, to be trapped in their own trap, they will not harm another human any more, as their permanent wounds will remind them to take a better path in their lives..."
"Sensei why dismantled the gun and threw the pieces in the sewer?"
Asks Joan this time...
"If that gun in the past, had fired a shot and injured or killed somebody, then, with my own fingerprints on it, I could be in trouble, drugging along with me, you both as well..."

One hour later

G.K.'s car, once more stopped out side the Cinemax Complex in Marousi.

Joan didn't kiss him goodbye after all, but they all just shook hands instead, exchanging their telephone and emails as well.

The girls waived at him when he did a U turn, passing in front of them. He in return flicked his lights and lifted his right hand.

The traffic lights just turned green and the white BMW went through them, swinging to the left at the first corner, disappeared before their eyes...

The two girls left behind, started an argument with loud voices, forgetting that the time was 1-30 in the morning, with Joan to be the domineering and the most demanding one.

If G.K. had to be listening to them he would of think twice before he picked up the phone to conduct either of them:

"Please Mary! Next time when we three meet, you mustn't come with us and do not phone or send him email. If by any change he conducts you, then you must tell him that you have an affair, which you do not want to break. After all, it's true, as you are almost engaged with that hairy Cypriot!"

"You also have an affair with that English iceberg.And you know something, I agree all the way with you when you call him an asshole! So, we may both have our reasons to change our boyfriends, but you or anybody else cannot stop me if I want to get in touch with him, or send him email, and because you irritated me, now, that I will go home, I am going to phone and if he isn't there, I will send him email!Bye – bye Joanna."

As Mary walks away to her car, Joan smiles and takes her mobile phone from her pocket, dealing G.K.'s number.

The man, in between the two girls, is still 1 kilometer away from his home as his mobile phone rings. He identifies Joan's name as he takes it out of his pocket.

"Hi Joanna! Are you both alright?"

"We are fine! We just had our daily argument, but this time You were the subject."

"What is the verdict? Am I guilty or not?"

To her silence, he understood the reason and he continues but with a deferent manner:

"Joanna! Nobody, even me, is worth the fighting between you and your friend and colleague. You have been friends for more than ten years and now again together at the Academy, even you are together on the weekends, let alone the hours of practice in the Dojo! Have a goodnight to both of you."

"No! No! Please, don't close the phone…"

Three days later

G.K. is sitting on his knees, on the floor of a large carpeted room. His hands are resting at his thighs. When you come closed to him you will realize that he is breathing slowly but deeply. His eyes are closed as he is in a deep coma. Behind him at the back of the room there is a door. That door opens slowly, very slowly, and a young girl appears.

She looks around and her beautiful blue - eyes come to rest on G.K.

With out disturbing him, quietly she sits down on an armchair. She waits a while and then as if reacting on a thought, she gets up slowly and with out making any noise picks up a poof. She lifts it high and walks towards G.K. When she is behind him, she throws herself and the poof into direction of G.K's head. With the force that she generates, she ends up on the…floor.

She screams with a shock and short breath as surprisingly she didn't find G.K's head. As she is on the floor, she looks to her left and she screams again as a bare foot hits out, almost touching her nose with a deep noise of the force of speed. That foot is the outside part of the ankle of the leg of G.K.; his voice brings her back to reality.

"I see that you like to make jocks."

He brings his leg back, gets up and helps the girl as well.

He puts on a pair of comfortable sandals oriental style, while the girl gazes in surprise.

Eventually she managed to talk, asking him of how he new that somebody was behind him.

G.K. with out saying anything takes her by her hand and directs her in the kitchen. On the table (In the center of the kitchen) was a Jar with orange juice and few classes. He pours a glass. While he is drinking (The girl refuses his request to help herself) he opens a cabinet and takes a plastic bottle with tablets in side. He takes one and swallows it with the juice. " Vitamins" he tells her. He fills the glass again with orange juice and takes the young girl back to the lounge. They both take a seat on the comfortable armchairs.

G.K. crosses both his legs on the armchair; he is wearing a black Karate pants and a black T-Shirt with very short sleeves.

The girl breaks the silence by asking once again of how he was capable of knowing she was there.

"Will you please tell me how you new that it was me?"

G.K. looks at her for a few seconds before he decides to talk:

"The many years that I spend with the Spirits of the Ancient Olympic Masters and Gymnasts, almost every one of them taught me how to develop a sixth sense."

"How come that one develops a sixth sense to that extent that can feel the presents of a human, I will very much like to know!"

"Every one had his methods, but it takes a lot of time and practice, so why don't you tell me first of what made you to come and see me with out phoning me?"

"First, Dad wants you to come home for something that concerns you, and second, I wanted to surprise you, but after this experience I will think it twice to surprise you again!" G.K. tells her to wait while he had a shower.

## CHAPTER EIGHT

G.K. was driven at a slow speed his white BMW; rolling along the road with the young girl next to him. Her name is Elpida (Hope) and is the girl whom he saved on the Mt. Olympus…

She once again begs him to tell her more about the sixth sense. She is so persuasive that G.K. decides to explain to her, at least theoretically.

"To reach the maximum standard of developing the sixth sense, first of all you have to antitoxic your self from the cancer of the Cities pollution. Another wards, you have to be as near to the nature as possible, without the noises and disturbances. Also, and the most important is; you have to exercise your body to that extent that you can conquer pain. The smallest injury from practice or from fighting, distorts the mind with the result the body cannot be relaxed to allow the blood vessels to flow easily…"

The car now enters the center of Athens and in few minutes they arrived at Elpidas Fathers office.

G.K. and Elpida are sitting on two armchairs opposite her Father (The Government Agent), which his code number is A5.

"You asked me over the phone to try to find the Orphanage that you were before you disappeared. It wasn't that difficult as those days there aren't many in Athens. This is the address."

A5 gives G.K. the address and telephone number.

G.K. takes the paper into his hands with excitement.

"I have more news for you!" The Government Agent tells G.K.

"You have a Mother and a Step Sister!"

"What!" Both G.K. and Elpida shouted.

"Yes it's true! Your Mother is alive and leaves in America, in Boston. She has been married to a Greek - American. She is very rich! They have a Daughter about 16 years old. Every year your Mother comes to Greece searching for your whereabouts. Some times your Mother comes alone and as from the time that she arrives in Athens until she departures, she is searching for you all over Greece, because she cannot accept that you are not alive!"

Suddenly dead silence is in the office of A5, if a needle drops on the carpeted floor, it could be heard by the 3 humans where are looking at each other with stunning surprise. Even A5 could not believe of what he is reading (From a fax paper).

The tensed atmosphere is eventually broken by G.K.:

"Why you are telling me all this? Why you went and investigated something that ..."

"I understand of what you want to tell me!" Said A5, interrupting him.

"Maybe it would be better if I never told you about your Family because if you didn't know it, you could be concentrated more of what you swore and learned, so, as from now on you will start looking for them and when you will find them then eventually develop a weak spot in your way to fight crime... Remember G.K., we maybe fight crime and we are ruthless about the bad elements, but when it comes to humans and to the family in particular, we (The United Nations) protect it at all costs and this is actually the reason why we fight crime, to protect the family, any family! We are not producing killing machines as wrongly has come out through the media to the public in the free World. Now that you know, then, everything depends on you!"

G.K. looks at A5 and tells him:

"Sir, whatever my private life will be in the future, if I will find my family or not, it will never change my promise to Goddess Athena and I will do everything in my Knowledge and Power to fight crime where ever comes from!"

A5 smiles happily. He looks upon G.K. and like he remembers something, tells him quickly:

"I forgot to tell you that your Mother and Sister are coming to Athens next week for their annual holiday. My Agent in Boston informed me last night!"

Next Day

G.K. stops his car; he looks through the window at the other side of the road of the well maintain old building.

He parks and walks across the road. He rings the bell of a door - gate and when it opens, he enters, closing it behind him.

He walks towards the receptionist.

Behind the desk a young girl is seating and talking on the phone to some Parent…

G.K. takes time to look around and memories come into his mind as very little things have changed in the `entering area area. While he is looking at a picture on the wall he noticed a Lady at her early sixties walking towards him, ready to pass him.

G.K. strait a way recognizes her, because he loved her like a Mother, as he never had, nor even met, his own Mother…

Before she passed him, he comes in front of her and tells her:

"Hello Mrs. Maria. Don't you recognize me? You haven't changed a bit! You look younger than ever!"

The old Lady looks at him in surprise but she smiles anyway, and while she analyzes him tries to picture his face… but she has forgotten her damn glasses in her office…

"If you could tell me your name, I will definitely remember you!"

G.K. ignores her question by telling her:

"It was a long time ago when I was one of your favorite boys who gave you the most troubles of doing dangerous tasks…placing my life in danger, when I was jumping even from one tree to another (Only two trees were those days in the Orphanage).

The Lady comes closed to his face and tells him with tears in her eyes:

"My boy! Twenty - one years ago, a tragedy happened at the Mount Olympus and my best boy, little George, disappeared in front of all the Teachers and Children, even in front of me…"

G.K. wants to interrupt to tell Mrs. Maria that:

<I am your little George. I am not dead; remember when I save the Cat from the tree and you told me that one day I would be `Protector of the Weak` and you nursed my finger that was bleeding…>, but he stops his thoughts as Goddess Athena enters his mind and tells him, `not to say it! `

G.K. looks at the young girl at the reception desk where by now she has stopped talking over the phone; opened her brown eyes and her mouth wide, when she is watching the ever melancholic and serious Care - Taker of the Orphanage, to cry in front of a strange man…

He turns his eyes to Mrs. Maria and tells her that he remembers the incident as he was also at the Mount Olympus:"You know Mrs. Maria, I will not be surprised if George is alive and will visit you one day at the

Orphanage… could I see the `garden` once more, please?
"

"It will be O.K., I suppose" Mrs. Maria said, and with out noticing the meaning of G.K, s words, she walks away with her eyes looking on the floor, shaking her head and wiping her tears, but…suddenly she stops and tells the girl to go to her office and fetch her glasses…
"Quickly! Quickly".
While the girl runs to her office, the old Lady is watching G.K. where he is getting out of the building.
When the girl comes, the old Lady waits until he is out in the garden, where now is much – much larger than before, with more than one hectare in size and twenty more trees and flowers in and around it. As for the play grounds, were designed to copy a small part of the Disncy Land…
G.K. pretends that he hasn't `feel` her coming and he looks around the magnificent garden, which is the only part that has been really changed since his time…
He made a pledge of offering to the `house` a swimming pool and a Tennis Court, so the orphan boys and girls, where are now were attending school classes, will have some fan and do some exercises as well. Also, he would of ask his Shihan – Master George Karavidas, to make a time and send somebody twice a weak to teach them his Art…"I will come as well" said talking to himself.

The old Lady is behind him, with her glasses on:
"Young man, what are your name and your surname? You didn't tell me, did you?"
All this time, G.K. is fighting with his conscience of not telling her, because, although he learned that he has a very rich Mother, which now explains the reason why he had so many expensive cloths, books, c.d. tape recorders, computer, even had a genuine Rolex; and if the DVD and

the Play Station would have been inverted, he would of have them all, plus Internet...but not his Mother and Father! But if his Mother was that rich, why she left him in the Orphanage? Why she didn't take him from there? What happened to his Father? He could give away all of those unnecessary `accessories` for a Mother and Fathers hug. For a Home! For a Family!

With all of these sad thoughts in his mind, couldn't tell Mrs. Maria his really name. Not until he had all the answers from his very Mother who will definitely meet her next week!

While he was thinking, the old Lady grabs him from his left arm and takes him few meters at the left side of the building, as she noticed the receptionist could see them through the window of the office:

"Mrs. Maria, I cannot tell you my name yet, although I feel very sorry about George's disappearance, as I was one of his closed friends. I even remember him when he did all those amazing things... he was a natural acrobat...I remembered when he had tied two ropes and while he was jumping from one tree to the other, imitating Tarzan, he fall on the ground and injured his arm..."

The old Lady takes him again from his left arm and directs him to the area that the injury occurred:

"Can you remember in which arm he was injured, because I keep forgetting," said Mrs. Maria guiltily, looking at his face behind her glasses, watching even every blink of his eyes...

"To his left arm" said G.K. without thinking, falling in to the trap of the clover Mrs. Maria, as that time of the accident, George was only by himself, because it was a sleeping time for the children, thus, nobody else except him would remember the accident of which arm he was injured...

Before realizes his mistake, she grabs his left arm again, but this time not to take him anyway, but to lift his sleeve up…

Into his effort to do a somersault and grab the second rope, it was then when he injured his left arm; the Doctors at the hospital had to put 20 stitches on it, leaving a ten centimeters scar for the rest of his life…

Both were speechless, looking at the scar, where it looked like a thin - red line, across his wrist.

The grown up George, out of the 21 hard years of education of mind and body, ether with the Ancient Spirits or with the leaving Master, never had any acting lessons, but he learned from his Greek - South African Master, that:

`Into the Pure World of Athletics' cannot go along with the Hypocrisy, Lie, Dishonesty and Fraud…`

Thus, G.K. gently removes his arm from Mrs. Maria and with a sudden move; he takes her into his arms, squishing her, calling her: Mother!

Few minutes later

With eyes still wet, they both finally are seated comfortably in the office of Mrs. Maria.

Although she has two grown up children of her own closed to G.K.'s age, she cannot hid her feelings about him, as she always had him in her heart, like he was one of her own:

"So, little George, will you tell me where were you all these years, making your Mother and all of us who loved you, to worry, thinking that you were dead?"

G.K. made up his mind of what to tell her:

"Mrs. Maria, if I tell you the real true story, of how it started and where I ended up, not only you will never believe me, but I will place yourself and me, in a great danger, if..."

In to her suggestion of interrupting him, he waives at her not too, as he understands of what she is going to ask him:

"For the time being, I will tell you what ever is necessary for you to know. Also, the same I will tell my Mother and her Daughter when hopefully I will meet them this Sunday...Oh! Mrs. Maria, please don't tell my Mother when she comes to visit you, that I am alive..."

"What!" She interrupts him. "Your Mother, for the last 21 years, she is half dead. She only `breaths` because she still has a hope that you are still alive, and you are telling me not to tell her? I should of phone her right away!"

G.K., calmly talks to the woman he only new for a Mother:

"Mrs. Maria, do you think I want to torture my Mother? Do you think that I do not have the feelings of a Son towards his Mother? The main reason that I do not want you to tell her is that, I want to see and feel by myself, like I felt for you when I saw you earlier in the corridor. If that Mother is worthy to have the divine title belongs only to the one who sacrifices herself for her child, no matter what!"

He looks at her to see if he had persuaded her and carries on:

"I also wanted to surprise her! Please, let me do it `my` way."

Five minutes later

G.K. comes out of the Orphanage and prepares to walk across the road to his car.

Suddenly a Motorbike came out of the parking area, where at the same time a very old woman in her seventies, walks along side and about ten meters in front of the Motorbike, with a handbag in her left hand.

The Lady is completely unaware of the Cyclists with a black helmet who accelerates, coming towards her from behind.

When comes closed to the Lady, he slows down and snatch the bag with his right arm, where her pension of 300 euro she just took from the bank was in it.

The slow down time was his grave mistake as he did not see G.K. where like a lightning takes a large step closing the gap and when the thug happily tries to speed up, he receives a round house kick from G.K's right leg on to his face, on the helmet. The angle between G.K.'s leg and the thug's helmet was 90 degrees, which means the thief had to pass with the bag in front of G.K…

The impact of the force was so hard that sends him somersaulting backwards with the helmet falling out of his head, running on the road, making a passing - by car to brake heavily but couldn't avoid the impact with the helmet. As for the motorbike, it skidded on the road and after doing one big somersault, strikes the side of the pavement and stops, making a squeaking noise.

G.K. quickly picks the bag up, then, turns his body around, doing something to the bag and gives it to the old Lady, touching her hair with his hand.

Before he went to his car, he looks at the assailant where he lies unconscious on the tar road next to the pavement. The position that he has taken on the road, it looks like he has a broken right leg, just under his knee…

"That is your punishment," said G.K. walking to his car. He starts quickly and speeds a way because people are coming to the scene, with a Police car approaching as well.

The old Lady stoned of what happened, looks at the assailant on the ground unconscious and G.K.'s car moving away; she shakes her head talking to herself.

"Oh God I think I am dreaming."

She opens her bag to see if her pension is still in there and…to her pleasant surprise, in front of her face, and on top of everything else, were two bank notes of 500 euro…with her pensions money of 300 euro, intact underneath them.

She closes her bag quickly as she sees a Police car stops behind the unconscious man.

One of the two policemen gets out of the car before even stops and started directing the cars, while unsuccessfully try to tell the people around to go away…

The other police officer gets also out and went to the old Lady where she is still standing in the middle of the road, holding tight her bag with both her hands…

He asks her politely to tell him of what exactly happened and if she had recognized the man who attacked the unconscious cyclist?

"This bag-snatcher attacked me! He took my bag with all of my pension's money that I just took from the bank. Thanks God, he sent me an Angel to save me… bye – bye; and before the Police Officer asks her anymore questions, the old Lady started walking away, faster than her age, clinching her bag with both her arms.

## CHAPTER NINE

A week later, early afternoons

The International Airport of Athens calls El. Venizelos (In the name of the late Great Politician) is one of the busiest Airports of Europe and not only the safest but the most modern as far as technology is concern.

People are coming and going by the thousands every day, right through the year...

We can now listen's the announcer informing all people where are waiting for the arrivals from Rome to tell them in Greek and Italian that:

"Alitalia; flight 345 from Rome has now touched down..."

G.K. is standing in front of the large electronic board that is fixed high up on the wall, looking for the flight from Boston. When he sees the number of the flight and the time schedule, he looks at his wristwatch and talks to himself.

"Another ten minutes."

If someone could fill his pals, then, surprisingly would tell that this man with all the skills and scientific education behind him, could not control his agony to ease and make his heart beating bellow 65 beats per minute as usually were, but now was definitely beating over 80 beats!

While he is still talking in side his mouth, he twists in his hands a photo of two women:

"My Mother after all these years"

He takes a deep breath trying to be calm. The announcer brings him back to his high-heart bitts as she says:

"American Airways, flight number 4144 from Boston, has now touched down…"

He didn't need anything else to ensure him that his Mother was already in Athens.

After a while, the first few people started coming out, making G.K. to move from where he was to another spot so he could see them properly…

Suddenly he saw the two coming out, rolling their trolleys with their language. He followed them at distance.

His Mother age about 50 years old. She looks slim with a body of a Professional Dancer. She moves very positively and at the same time very lightly, like a mature Cat, pushing the trolley with a Suitcase and a large traveling bag. Along with her Mother was his step Sister. She appears very young and very beautiful (Brunette like her Mother) with two plats hanging in front of her. They moved out of the building and a driver comes out of a Mercedes car, greets them like he new them, taking their luggage and place them in the trunk, then he opens the rear door and let them in. Then, he takes the drivers seat and the car moves away with out of course notice

G.K's wet eyes.

Although he couldn't see properly, he managed to see the Customers - Courtesy Sign of Hilton Hotel, at the driver's side of the Mercedes.

Next day (About 10 am)

G.K. finds a place to park and comes out of his car, with intention to visit the Hilton Hotel. He is about 200 meters away on the other side of the road where he looks and admires the oldest of the few International Hotels scattered around Athens.

He walks slowly and while he is looking around carefully in case he sees his mother and sister, also he guides himself to the scenery around him as he hasn't seen it before.

Because of the many years that he was away from Athens and also before he disappears on the mount Olympus, they, at the Orphanage, never brought him in that part of the city. They only took the children to some Archeological sites.

He was still standing on the pavement when he fills a man watching him, trying to come closed...

G.K. doesn't get alert as when was in danger, but his highly developed six senses, tells him to be careful.

Suddenly he stops and turns his face to his left. Of what he sees is a man where for some reason he has lost his job but he would try everything to support his family. Another word, the man was an amateur crook, where in this case he was after innocent tourists to try to sell them...

"Sir," the amateur crook calls on G.K., coming closer.

"Are you looking for something?"

Some of this kind of crooks are harmless, but can be a pain in the neck if persistent...

"Yes I am." said G.K. smiling.

"And what is that?" Asked the man not sure of himself any more, of the whereabouts of this strange Greek or Italian tourist.

"The Hilton Hotel"

"What?"

"Yes my friend. That Hilton Hotel, over there!" said G.K. smiling again.

The man understood that G.K. wasn't a tourist, but... oh well, he always had an alternative.

He opens his long overcoat reviling some watchers hanging from the left and right side.

"I have a video camera as well, and if you want a young girl…"

G.K. when he heard the last suggestion, about offering him a young girl… he made an extra effort not loose control, but decided to stop this man, and at the same time teaching him a lesson about human respect…

He extents his left open palm and strikes the man on a certain spot of his solar plexus, controlling the strike of not to break any ribs, just to cut his breath a little.

The man (at his forties and taller of G.K.), apart of the shock he had, as he didn't see anything coming; felt a sharp pain in his stomach, but… his wind was blocked inside his chest, made him difficult not only to breath but to stand up…

G.K. grabbed him quickly before people recognized of what was happening and takes him to the edge of the public garden which were about two meters away. He then places his right arm behind the man's back and felt the right lung. By using his fingers and some pressure, he energizes faster the oxygen into his veins, thus, reviving the man's breath, but of course the pain was still there…

G.K. released him. He then takes out of his jackets pocket one hundred euro and gives it to him:

"Take this and you must promise me that you will go and find a decent job! You look healthy! I could be a Policeman, and…"

"But you are definitely not" said the crook, moving backwards, afraid of been attacked again, still holding the one hundred euro bill.

G.K. cannot help of smiling, but when he was going to ask him of how he understood that, the man already was telling him:

"Your accent looks like you are a Greek from abroad, and definitely you were not born in Greece!"

"You are hundred percent… wrong, as I was born in Piraeus, but I grew up in… another Country… Now, because you didn't promise me that you will go and find a decent job, thus, in this case you are loosing your profit..."

Before he finishes his last word, he snaps the bill with his left hand.

To the astonished crook, G.K. makes few steps to go away, but he returns back and asks him:

"Do you have any children?"

From his grimace of his face, G.K. realizes that he has found his weak spot.

"Of course you don't want them to learn that you are not only a beggar and a crook, but dirty as well, as you are also mixed up with prostitutes. Are you?"

As the man is in no position to answer; G.K., decides right here and right now, on the pavement, which is other side of the Hilton Hotel, to put this man on the 'right road', not only for the sake of doing something humanitarian, but for the sake of this man's children!

"You know what? From an angry Tourist or a Greek, you could be in a serious trouble, even ending up in prison? I will give you a change of a lifetime, and an opportunity to make your children and your wife to be proud of you, but you must have knowledge of some gardening and have a valid driver license..."

<Lefteris (Teri) Yannoulis; since the birth of his second child, swore to God that he will get a decent job, to offer his children not only a proper home and security, but to be proud of their Father, like his brother in-law where he was working in the Athens Municipality as a Gardener.

He (Teri) was unlucky because he had to drop out of the two year agriculture course, just only the last quarter of the second year, as he had to work to support his family, but the money he was earning from the building construction company, wasn't enough to pay all the

George Karavidas, G.K.

expenses at home, thus, he tried everything that brings extra money...>

Teri cannot believe of what he just heard, that this man offered him not only a permanent job, but something that he loved it so much...

He mobilizes all his courage and asks G.K. if he was not joking?

"No, I am not joking at all. So, what do you say? Do you accept?"

"Yes! Yes, I accept!"

G.K., somehow satisfied of himself that his first mission of human judging was going fine; asks the man to tell him his name and little bit about him.

Teri, with out even breathing, tells G.K. of what we just wrote above, plus little more, of his love for gardening...

"All set! I forgot to tell you that you will have you own home where you can even cultivate your own fruit and vegetables as well, if you wish of course. Here is my card!"

G.K. gives him a card that writes: Diplomat.

"With one condition" said G.K. penetrating the eyes of this little crook, but other wise a good family man:

"As you your self will be making the working hours in the house and the garden; you will promise me that you will finish your Agricultural course"

"I promise you Sir, and I will never disappointed you and you can trust me with my life! As long as I will get out of this kind of Cancer I am in; making my wife and my children to live in anxiety and fear."

"You can come tomorrow morning at ten o clock and I will arrange the transportation of your furniture..."

"Don't worry about that. I have a friend with a truck that will do it." said Teri. "Thank you Sir"

The two men shook hands.

G.K. walks and stops at the pedestrian crossing, waiting for the green light to appear.

At this very moment where the Sun shines and the well known Grecian blue skies are free of clouds; all of a sudden a thunder sounds, makes the people that are in Athens to lift their heads up as they missed the lightning; but the sky makes them happy by another lightning, followed again by another thunder... but... the rain never comes.

G.K. looks up and smiles. If somebody could penetrate his brain, would have seen and listen to Goddess Athena telling him:

"Well done Giorgo (George)! Well done!

Few minutes later, G.K. enters the foyer of the Hotel.

While looking around he is trying unsuccessfully of not to be noticed from the people where are customers or workers. The reason for that is, apart of been well dressed, he moves different of every other human. He looks like his feet are barely touching the thick carpet. On the other hand, when the one leg is lifted, the other appears to be fixed on the ground with perfect balance...

He takes a seat one of the comfortable Armchairs of the large living room. He nodes to one of the waiters and when he comes closed, gives him an order of a lemon – tea and an apple pie!

When the waiter walks away to execute the order, G.K. noticed at the reception something unusual going on...

There are some people requiring and arguing with the Manager of the Hotel. They appeared to be Italian businessmen and apparently there was a mistake about a reservation of a suite.

The Manager tries desperately to calm them down as their voices are very loud and they all speak together (they are three gentlemen).

The Managers politeness, instead of calm them down are getting them more furious and one of them (the biggest in size), pushes, the smaller in size Manager, forcing him to go back. On his effort to gain balance, the poor Manager opened his arms and while he was pedaling backwards he strikes a Lady customer on her shoulder from the back and both fall on the carpet.

The Lady though, isn't falling as the Manager did, but in spite of the unexpected force on her back of her shoulder, she managed to do a Judo rolling fall and before she gets back on her feet she jumps on the air twisting her magnificent body 180 Degrees and lands facing the big Italian with her fists closed in front of her chest. She is wearing white Slacks.

The Italians fat jaw gets fatter as his moth opens downwards from surprise, but he is not the only one with his mouth wide open…

That was G.K., where he gets up, approaching the scene, as the Lady where has surprises every body with her ability and skill of a Martial Artist, is non other than his very own Mother.

As the Lady (G.K's Mother) sees no danger, she lets her arms down.

After she looks at the Manager and the big Italian, then she realizes of what happened and without hesitation she walks and helps the Manager where he is getting up, shacking his head left – right.

She looks at the Italian again who is now talking to one of the other two. She walks and stops in front of him telling him politely in clean English to apologize to the Manager.

The big Italian looks at her as he looks at Sofia Loren, then he whispers something in Italian to his friends with a nodding smile. He then turns his head to the beautiful Lady and with broken English tells her:

"Lady, you look so beautiful, why do not let me apologize to you, instead of this ugly bastard?" pointing at the Manager.

She looks at the Manager and she realizes that he is in no position to talk back to the Italian, but he talks to one of the attendants of the Hotel instead, most probably to tell him to phone the Police.

Before she talks to the hot-tempered Italian, he attempts to touch her check with his left hand. She waits until his hand is closed to her face; then with a quick snap, strikes his arm with her left palm away of her face and she kicks him, with a direct warning kick - like to his right shin. The big man screams from pain and tries to touch his right leg with his arms, but he gets a smack from her right arm instead, pushing him backwards and she finishing him off by firing a

Back - kick to his stomach with her right leg. The kick was perfectly executed (not so hard though) and the big Italian was forced to land in the hands of his two friends holding his stomach but he still conscious and very very angry.

She looks at him with her dark brown eyes waiting for his reaction with her arms erected at her side.

The man, apart of the pain she caused him, he had his pride to restore, and with a sudden move of both his hands gets free from his friends, ignoring their advices to stop, as he is making a full of himself...

He brings both his hands on top of his trousers and pulls out his leather belt with a large buckle. He twists the one end around his right wrist and leaves the other end with the buckle hanging out. He starts moving while swearing in Italian Language.

The other two, shouts at him again, telling him not to do it, and when the one tries to stop him, he gets a hard push, sending him in the arms of the other, who shakes his head in despair.

If these two couldn't stop their friend, possible because they were afraid of him, G.K. is already there, passing them and before the man lifts his belt to strike his Mother, he grabs with his left hand the right side of the big mans neck, pinching a nerve. The man is screaming again, but this time is very painful making him going down to his knees, still screaming.

While still pinching the nerve, G.K. whispers in his ear in Italian language, telling him to apologize to the Lady!

The man with out hesitation apologizes in English.

While the man did his duty and apologized, G.K's eyes met with his Mothers...

The two of them, Mother and Son, are looking at each other and for a few seconds it looks like there was nobody else around. This kind of ecstasy though, lasted only 5 seconds as she springs forward telling him in Greek:

"Look out..."

G.K.'s Mother does not knowing this mans ability at all, she only hopes her Son could be alive somewhere in Greece and one day she will find him. But this man out of nowhere, is coming to her rescue, reminds her of...

One of the Italians runs to hit G.K. from behind with an umbrella (he is holding it all the time, because it was raining in Milan) with the metal handle at the end of it.

G.K. moves his body to the right and at the same time strikes the umbrella with his left palm circular ways towards the head of the kneeling man, thus, making the force faster and harder. The umbrella land on the unfortunate big mans head where he screams again, but this time blood comes out of the temple (right side) of his head.

The attacker before realizes what he has done, he gets a single open palm strike to his face from the right hand and a round house kick to his head (as he is going backwards) from the right leg of G.K., sending him to rest on the carpeted floor of the Hotel. The third man, looks of what happened to his friends and decides to keep quiet.

Mother and Son looks at each other again, but this time are at one meter apart, but again before anyone says a single word to each other, somebody sounds at the back, that the Police is coming!

The warning, makes G.K. to realize the importance of avoiding the Police, although now he had legal documents, did not want though to be questioned for his present at the Hotel.

He bows politely to his Mother and walks towards the exit while the Police are coming inside.

G.K.'s Mother is astonished.

When some one could come closed to her and could see the expression of her face and read her mind, she would tell:

"This man would be seen more of me in the very near future!"

Few minutes later

G.K. enters his car with mixed fillings: He is very happy, not only to see his Mother for a first time in his life, but to see her in action as a Martial Artist? His unhappiness was, because he had to strike (although controlled) two Italian business men...

Inside his mind came the time where he had many conversations with his Master in South Africa about Countries and People. When (the Master) was talking with so much respect about the Ancient Greeks, he had the same respect and admiration of the Ancient Romans too.

Frequently he was telling G.K. about the resemblance to the Greek Nation where were: The Italians and the Spaniards. He could not understand why these 3 Nations do not speak the same language. If he had it, he would start bringing the Politicians together (including Cypriots of course)...

## CHAPTER TEN

### Next morning

Mrs. Karanikos - Georgiou (G.K.'s Mother or Mrs. K.) parks her car and walks towards the orphanage building.

She knocks the door. Mrs. Maria opens, as she was waiting for her.

The two Ladies, embrace each other and Mrs. Maria takes Mrs. Karanikos inside.

They are now sitting in the office and after the normal chat, the host Lady tells the visitor:"So you are back again to look for your Son I presume?"

"Yes Mrs. Maria, and as long as I live, I will keep looking for him! He must be a grown up man by now."

"Mrs. K. I promised you to look and try to report to any unusual things or unusual inquires by people coming here from time to time. But since last year where you were here I have nothing worth telling you, except the normal inquires."

Mrs. K. looks at Mrs. Maria with sympathy and while she gets up, tells her:

"I don't know how to thank you for all the years where you are helping me and understand my agony. I am grateful to you for the rest of my life… You know where I am staying in Athens. If you heard or see anything that is worth investigating, then please do not hesitate to phone me."

Mrs. K. comes out of the building and starts walking towards her car when the door of the Orphanage opens and Mrs. Maria appears.

"You know Mrs. K.? A young man came here last week. He claimed that he was with us a long time ago. Also told me that he new little George and he believes he may still be alive..."Did you recognize him?" asked quickly G.K, s Mother."No I didn't (Mrs. Maria said in despair), but he remembered me by my name..." "Did he gave you any address or a telephone number?" Mrs. K. interrupts her again."Nothing!" she said again and she felt guilty, as she didn't ask him.

"He only wanted to look the back yard of the Orphanage, but the way he handled the Bag Snatcher..."

She explains to her that she watched him through the window.

"He looked like he new a lot about fighting or Karate or something..."

Artemis (G.K.'s Mother) embraces Mrs. Maria:
"You have no idea, how much you helped me!"

Five minutes later

In her car while drives towards the Hilton Hotel, she unfolds inside her mind the fight in the Hotel, while analyzes the last words of the old Lady:
"But the way he handled the bag snatcher..." "Bag snatcher?" She repeats again and again...

We see her coming inside the Hotel.

Without noticing anybody, she takes the lift to the 6th floor. She gets out and directs herself to number 611. She opens the door and enters the luxurious apartment.

On the carpeted floor her daughter Persa is doing stretching exercises. She is wearing a white Karate Uniform and a black belt around her trim waist.

The Mother greets her daughter and going strait to the phone. She presses a button and at the same time she picks up a telephone directory from underneath the table.While she is looking through the pages, she was murmuring…

"Newspapers, newspapers… oh, there you are!"

By the looks of it, she has found of what she was looking for and dials a number. Her Daughter is watching here very anxiously!

Next morning

G.K. is sitting on an armchair with his legs crossed. He holds a newspaper and he is talking to somebody on the phone. His voice sounds happily surprised of what he heard from the other side of the line.

"Yes I can see," G.K. said.

"There is no doubt that my mother wants to meet me. Yes I will go! I already have called and find out about the apartment they are staying. I will try not to reveal my identity, but it will be very difficult! Yes I will phone you. Thank you for the news; with out you I may not have seen it. Thank you again A5."

He replaces the receiver back and reads loudly the newspaper to himself.

"The Gentleman who helped me to overpower two men at the Hilton Hotel, requests to contact me at the same Hotel. I am very anxious to meet him and thank him personally"

G.K. is holding the newspaper for about a minute with his eyes fixed at nowhere.

He decides to move!

He lifts the receiver and he dials a number while looking at the newspaper's top right corner, where he had written with a pen the telephone and the apartment number of the Hilton Hotel.

While the telephone is ringing, G.K.'s tongue all of a sudden feels dry and he looks like he is not breathing properly. He talks to himself for he would prefer to fight with all the bad elements in the World, instead of...

The switchboard operator brings him back to reality.

"Hilton Hotel, can I help you?"

"Could you please put me through to room 116?"

"Certainly"

At last his Mother comes to the phone:

"Mrs. Karanikos speaking" "Hello Lady, I am the person who assisted you - as you call it-. I saw the ad in the newspaper about your request to meet me..."

G.K. heard himself to talk to his Mother and could not believe his ears of the calmness of his voice. Could be the so many years of heard practice? I suppose...

"Yes, yes!" His Mother interrupts his thoughts. "Thank you for replying to my request... You are full of surprises; first with your Martial Arts skill and now with your good English... Are you not Greek?"

G.K. tries to think before answering and decides to be cynical.

"I am Greek like you are; I also learned English like you did, Mrs. Karanikos."Mrs. K., although surprised again of how he learned about her Surname; never the less she asks him about it.

"Simply" G.K. replies. "The receptionist was very help full, although she told me of two surnames..."

"Will you please tell me your name?" The Mother asks, while softens her voice a little."Please leave it at that Mrs. Karanikos! For the time been you can call me G.K., and no questions ask, please!""O.K, O.K.," his Mother replied quickly, feared she would loose him from the line."Suit your self! Will you do me the honor to have lunch or dinner with my daughter and me? We like to meet you as we also involved in Martial Arts."

She said those words that easy, but inside her mind she insulted herself of been that hurry and possibly put her new friend in difficult position. She wanted to meet him desperately, as he could lead her to whereabouts of her Son...

G.K. has been prepared mentally, and to his Mothers surprise he accepts the invitation:

"It will be my pleaser Maam, but I will prefer not to meet you at the Hotel, if you don't mind?"

"No, I don't mind at all, she tells him quickly; do you have any other place in particular?" "No I don't, but our Country has so many Archeological sites worth seen; why then we don't take a drive to Piraeus, then, take the Flying Dolphin to Aegina Island...

"And visit the temple of Aphaia." His Mother ended. "Exactly," G.K. said gladly. "You know that Aegena, apart of its colorful History, has produced many Athletes where were Champions at the Ancient Olympics...

"Mainly for Pagratio," she ended again.

Please note: Pagratio was an Art of fighting, started at 648 b. C. in the Ancient Olympia. It was a combination of Wrestling and Boxing, fight to the finish...

The Author many years ago in South Africa (1973) introduced a fighting Art where has its Roots and Philosophy at the Ancient Pagratio.

For more information, please look at the last pages.

"You are now surprised, me!" G.K. said. "Apart of your Martial Arts skill, you know a lot about our Ancient History as well. Do you have any more surprises Mrs. K.?"

They kept talking about the Ancient Greek History, while they organized of how and where to meet:

Mother and Daughter will call their driver to take them to the Harbor of Piraeus, where the `Flying Dolphins` are leaving every half hour, and G.K. will meet them there with his car.

## CHAPTER ELEVEN
3 hours later

Mother and Daughter arrived first at the beautiful site of Freatida (East of the main harbor of Piraeus) where the fast moving Boats, call, Flying Dolphins, are operating mainly towards the Aegean Islands, and Aegina is one of them.

After Mrs. K. discussed with the driver what time to pick them up in the afternoon, the Mercedes leaves and the two are walking towards the ticket box.

Both are wearing shorts, thus, their trimmed bodies are exposed to the hot weather, but also to the two `hot` Mediterranean young Greeks where are watching them.

The young men are coming from behind and without thinking that they could understand Greek, they started talking between themselves loud enough:"Nice buttocks," said the one with chestnut curly hair."I prefer the older one," says the other with a dark red hair. "She looks to be much more experience!"

Mrs. K. and her daughter who understands everything they are saying pretends the opposite and tries to ignore them.

Artemis (the Mother) says something to Persa in English and walks by herself to the ticket box. She purchased 3 tickets to Aegina and pays with euro. Puts the tickets in her bag and turns around towards her daughter.

She sees the two young men trying to make friends with her. The Mother smiles but not happily and she shakes her head left right while approaching them slowly. Her daughter though, looks very angry, and she talks to them in very good Greek:

"I understood everything you said! Now that you preserved yourselves at your best, can you leave me alone?"

She looks at them with her eyes wide open, and although her voice is very soft and kind, at the same time is demanding and will take no more nonsense!

The young men instead of leaving her alone, they come closer to her...

Persa throws her bag on the ground, while moving her right leg back and assumes a fighting stance, with her arms in front of her body, closing her fists.

"Gentlemen please live me alone!" She repeats again.

The young men were surprised to see that this foreign Greek girl she is not like the others; she really wants to be left alone.

Mrs. K. is already close to them and she also tells them to leave!

These two young Mediterranean men-boys, they mean no harm to her; they only wanted some kind of adventure, thinking they were tourists and they wanted to have a good time...

As they felt a bit embarrassed then, the one with the curly her, apologized to them and tell his friend:

"Let's go... Let's go!!

They started walking away with their shoulders and head down with out saying a word to each other.

Young Persa brings her left foot back, parallel to the other and take a deep breath to relax, bringing her arms down too, while her Mother is giving her bag.

The Mother embraces her with left arm around her shoulder and tells her to go and seat on one of the benches (which are reserved for the passengers of the boats) waiting for their new friend:

"Let's hope that he is not the same as them." said Persa, still angry, as she cannot understand this Mediterranean kind of courting.

From the other side, at the car park, G.K. is watching everything with a smile.

He comes out of his car locking the driver's door; automatically the alarm is engaged, and walks towards his Mother and Sister.

They all shake hands and `officially` introduced themselves: G.K.with his initials, his Mother as Artemis Karanikos – Georgiou and his Sister as Persephone (Persa) Georgiou.

As they do not have any more time to loose and every body comes aboard the Fly Dolphin, they walk to the boat.

The engines are starting … Very carefully and slowly the Captain maneuvers the boat.

As gradually speeds up the Engines, the `Dolphin` looks like its not touching the water.

The two women are seating next to each other, talking and enjoying the scenery that Greece is well known for its natural beauty of the Mediterranean sea, where almost all the inhabitant Islands are breath taking, thus, makes the Tourists to come back again and again.

Mrs. K., behind her blue sunglasses, although she enjoys the scenery, her eyes are looking at G.K. as well...

Her heart beats furiously as she tries to have a good look at his face with out been noticed, but not only he is looking to the other side of the boat, thus, makes it more difficult, but all the time he is wearing this damn dark glasses as well...

G.K. is also ecstatic of the view and also his emotions are the same as with his Mother, the only different is, that he knows who his Mother is, but he doesn't know if she is worth the love and affection...

With their minds to each other, plus the beauty of nature, Mother and Son did not realized of what happened around them inside the boat.

Alongside of the two women (Mother and Daughter), are sitting two Albanians, where the way they were looking at their bags, their jewelry of their neck and wrists, also the way they were talking between themselves, while looking at the two Women and from examine G.K.; then, one could say that these two are there for trouble of some short! Certainly they weren't admires of the beauty of the scenery as hardly they look over the sea.

The normal time to Aegina with the Dolphin is about 35 minutes of beautiful nature of water and land.

Eventually they arrived on the Island.

They disembark and started walking towards the main road, with out noticed the other passengers who are coming from behind them.

People are moving all over the place; the open Cafes and Restaurants are preparing for the days rush, which will be full of Tourists (mainly Greeks) where coming from Athens and Piraeus to swim, to visit the Archeological sites, the Pistachio nut trees, the Lemon Tree Forest, etc. Also to enjoy the traditional Greek Cuisine that is the most tasteful in the World.

A lot of Greeks from the mainland and also from abroad are coming for the Church of Agios (Saint) Nectarios, which makes a lot of miracles and wonders for its Pilgrims.

For a first time Mother and Son had a change to have a good look at one another, as they took their glasses off. That happened after they rent a Monipos (a Cart with a single Horse that serves as an attraction for the Tourists, for the simple reason, to avoid the use of their motor car) and now they are occupying the single back seat, with Persa sitting next to the Rider. While strolling along the beach - front of the center of Aegina and both loaded with sentimentality, they didn't see the two Albanians entering a white Mercedes and followed them from safe distance...

After about 10 minutes of ride over the main road, they arrived at the 'Faros' Restaurant where they were going to have breakfast.

The polite waiter suggested a table under shadow with a view of the sea.

Please note: The beginning of summer in Greece is dry and some times very hot. At this period, the temperature is about 30c.

Another waiter comes to take the order.

They all order breakfast, of eggs and sausages, with orange juice...

Mrs. K. decides to take her bracelets and necklace off, telling Persa to do the same. After Persa gives her Mother all her Jewelry, she (the Mother) opens her bag and places them in side. She hangs the bag on to her chair. On her finger though, she still keeps her 4-karat diamond ring, which is the most expensive item of them all.

Again, nobody paid any attention of the two Albanians where they were dropped about 50 meters off the Restaurant, and now are occupying a table behind them. Almost at the same time a speedboat comes and rests close to the Restaurant with out dropping an Anchor...

Mrs. K. breaks the silence. "You know G.K., I am coming to Greece every year for more than 20 years. I came once with my late husband as well! Some times, like now, I bring my daughter with, but most of the time I am coming alone. You know that, every time I come, I feel the same excitement like I see Greece for a first time."

G.K. looks at her with out saying anything, as she continuous like she is talking to herself.

"I have been almost all over Greece, looking and asking people, searching and inquiring at every Institution; also the Red Cross, News Papers, T.V..." "Mother" Persa interrupts her. "Mr. G.K. does not want to know our problems!"

G.K. looks at both of them, he still keeps quiet, says nothing. He prefers not too, as he is very weak emotionally and if he asks questions will make them suspicious.

Mrs. K. asks him to forgive her for getting carried away:"You know, I am looking for my Son that I lost him 21 years ago from the orphanage... her eyes are getting wet. Her daughter embraces her around her shoulder and telling her again, to control herself and continuous by saying to her:"After all Mom he is a stranger, we just met him, he doesn't want to..."

G.K. cannot ignore them any more and he interrupts by saying to Persa:

"Miss Georgiou, your Mother doesn't bother me at all! Her story interests me very much and if I can help, I will!"

He turns to his Mother and tells her to continue.

Mrs. K. intents to carry on but other things are happening so quick, like in a movie turning the ever - friendly atmosphere of the Island to a terror, and all this happened in a broad daylight...The three are sitting in a manner where all are looking at the sea, with their backs to the other tables. On the right of G.K. is sitting his Mother with Persa next to her.

That time, a time of emotion, where he is not alert to feel the coming danger; that time, the 2 Albanians decided to strike, as all their plans were working fine...

The target of course was the bag of Mrs. K. with the jewelry and possible with a lot of money in side, including the diamond ring of course!They strike simultaneously at G.K. and his Mother. The bigger man goes behind her and grabs her hair with his left arm, strikes her on the neck with his right open palm, pushing – throwing her unconscious on to the arms of her daughter, thus, keeping Persa occupied by holding her Mother. That split of a second G.K. alerted his senses and slides his body to the left, out of the chair, thus, avoiding the iron - pipe, which the second Albanian uses to hit him over to his head.

The iron - pipe hits the empty metal table making a big bang, with the surprised Albanian to fall on the table, and before his face had a time to grin of pain, G.K. jumps high up, flying on the air towards the thug. At the same time he lifts his right elbow. On the downward way, he holds the thugs back with his left palm and he is ready to kill him by strike him with his elbow at the base of his neck, breaking his spine.

On that split of a second, Goddess Athena comes to his mind and commands him:

"No Kill! No kill!"

G.K. directs his elbow lower, towards the thugs left kidney...

The first thug missed his only change he had to run away with the bag, but, as of his main objective was the ring...so, when he stretches his dirty arm to snatch out of the finger of G.K.'s Mother, then; a deep bung behind his dry head from the instep of G.K.'s right foot, sends him to sleep, with a permanent damage of his neck. The force of the kick sends him also with his face flat on the table, on top of his compatriot, making them looking very funny with their buttocks exposed, asking for a good span...

G.K. now is very alert as he feels that the danger is still around. He looks at the two thugs where are unconscious but still cannot relax. He quickly turns around as he senses the danger from the sea.

As he turns his body left ways, he felt first and sees after… the speedboat that was afloat earlier and he did not paid any attention to it… to speed away.

He then turns to see his Mother.

All these happened in few seconds, but something about his Mother in his sister's arms worried him and he checks her pulse. He is getting 'no pulse'.

He brings her on her seat and comes close to her face… but nothing, no breathing…

He looks at his Mother, and like nobody was around he talks to her in Greek.

"No, God! Not now that I find her!"Persa, although shocked of what happened to her Mother, heard what he said and she looks at him with her eyes and mouth wide open;     managed     to     say     to     him… "Who are you? Please, save my Mother?"

G.K. without answering to his sister's question, and to the surprise of the people who are starting coming around looking at the two Albanians unconscious on the table and the woman unconscious on the chair; it was then, where with a sudden move of his left palm, cleans the table of the two dirty rats and quickly brings another table, to join them together.

On his way to the second table, an unfortunate plastic chair was in his path… the next second it was flying over the air and it landed half broken in the sea.

He then takes his Mother and places her flat on the two tables.

Every body now is watching G.K's effort to save his Mother, ignoring the two thieves who are on the ground, facing each other's face…

First, he opens her mouth to see if she hasn't swollen her tang. Then he lifts his right hand with a close fist and strikes her Sterno (chest) with a control punch; straight after that he places both his open palms on the same spot where he strike and pumps it few times. After that, he gives her the kiss of life by holding her nose with his two fingers. When he gets a change he talks to her:

"Please don't die! I am here now and I will never live you again! Please Goddess Athena, give me the power?"

And while carries on the respiration process, his thoughts went to his Grand Master when he was teaching him of how to give life when no pulse...

To the surprise of the people, mostly to Persa where she heard everything, her Mother comes to life after the second attempt.

Artemis opens her eyes and the first thing that she sees is G.K.'s face. To her request of what had happened, G.K. instead of answering he thanks his Master George Karavidas of teaching him to save lives and also Goddess Athena...

Gently, like he is lifting a little baby, he helps his Mother to her feet. The people gathered around, applauded his effort, but G.K. had eyes and ears only for his Mother.

The Shopkeeper although not used to this kind of disturbances, managed to call the Police and a Police car with two officers are coming to the seen.

The waiter explains what happened.

The Policemen without hesitation calf the two dizzy robbers, where the waiter and two bystanders had lifted them up from the ground, holding them tight for the Police to come.

One of the Policemen tells G.K. that these two are from the Albanian Mafia, thus, he made a service to the Police and if he wanted to press charges against the thieves...

He gives him his card and tells him:

"I will leave the Law to punish them. You can say that you arrested them, but in case you need me for anything, then you can call me."The Police Officer in charge, at his late twenties, looks at the card and reeds loudly in good English:

"Private Investigator (International)"

"So, you are a college, so to speak?" said the other Police Officer...

With out any other questions, the two Policemen carried the Albanians in the car and driven a way to the Police station, where it is only few hundred meters away.

Mrs. K. is sitting again on the same chair as before and G.K. is sitting next to her, with Persa speechless and moving only her eyes, looking at her Mother and G.K., again and again.

With her emotions sky high, the Mother of both looks at G.K. as he touches her hair gently. She takes his hand and holds it in between her both hands, while she talks to him:

"You know G.K., you saved my life again, this time you brought be back from death and I cannot find words to thank you, but inside my heart I have the filling that you remind me of my Son. Same face, same futures, everything the same!"

G.K. decided that now is the right time to let out what actually wanted to ask her from the beginning.

"How long ago since you haven't seen your Son?" He asks by bringing his chair close to her.

At this crucial moment, the waiter decides to bring the breakfast.

While he is placing the plates with the juices and the mineral water on the table, he praises G.K. for his quick action against the thieves.

Although looks at the waiter, G.K. doesn't listen at all, as his concentration is to his Mothers answer. He is very interested to know if she is worthy to be a Mother and could share his secret as a `Protector of the Weak. `

"I haven't seen him since he was 10 years old. I heard the news of his disappearance at the Mount Olympos as they phoned me in New York from the orphanage…"

"Why you left him in the orphanage?" G.K. interrupts her.

"I didn't leave him!" She looks at him deep into his eyes, tries to find out the meaning of his words, but never the less she carries on:

"It's a long story, but I will try to be as quick as possible…"

"Mom" Persa interrupts her Mother.Mrs. K. turns her face towards her daughter."Yes darling"

Persa wants to tell her of what G.K. said earlier while she was almost dead,

"Its all right Mom, please carry on!"

Mrs. K. with out noticing anything continues:"I was telling you that I didn't leave my Son in the orphanage!" While she carries on, very emotionally, trying unsuccessfully to stop her tears coming out.

"I was 18 years old and my fiancé was 22 when he left for overseas. At that time I was 3 months pregnant, but I made a mistake and I didn't tell him about my pregnancy, as I wanted him out of love to send me a ticket to go to him to Africa.

"You mean the Father of your child is still alive?"

It was G.K.'s turn to interrupt her this time, but he did it with an unusual manner, unnatural to his character.

His Mother is not that naïve, but as it is so naturally for any human to be absorbed of his/her own story, so, she answers immediately with out `catching` the deep meaning of the question.

"I think so; but what difference does it make? "No it's nothing!" G.K. hurries to tell her. "Carry on! Sorry for the interruption, but please if you don't mind to tell me the reason why he left you? "

She looks at him again for a few seconds and carries on: "He didn't abandon me so to speak, but because he was posted as a Mechanical Engineer in South Africa or in Zimb…"

Before she finishes her word, G.K. jumps up interrupting her by saying:

"What did you say? South Africa? You say that my…I mean, your fiancé, went to South Africa?"

He realizes of what he just said, only when Goddess Athena tells his mind:

"Control Giorgo (George), Control yourself!"

G.K. drops on his seat and tries unsuccessfully to change the subject by telling his Mother:

"Sorry! Please carry on!"

She looks at him again and although she `forgives` him, she reserves the right to ask him many questions later on!

"I was telling you that, apart of South Africa he could be posted in Rhodesia (now Zimbabwe), because the Company had a brunch there. Come to think now, in case he was posted in Zimbabwe he could be in danger of all the unrests in those days between the Blacks and Whites…"

G.K. falls-fully thinking that he is in full control of himself, thus, asks his Mother a question without thinking of how he could react to the answer:

"What… was…the full name of your fiancé?"

She looks at him again, ready to ask him of why he so interested, but never the less, she answers his question:

"Although I do not see how his name could make any difference to the whereabouts of my child; his name was, I mean is, George Karavidas…"

"G.K. what happened to you?" mother and daughter asking simultaneously.

<G.K., is in no position to tell them, because he just learned that the person where he lived with and practiced for more than 10 years, with 6 and more hours per day in the Dojo... The person whom the first 3 years hated him so much, because made him having nightmares; making the `torture` of the first 10 years he had with the Spirits of the Ancient Olympic Champions and Gymnasts, to look like he had a camping holiday… The Master, where after the 3 years passed, when G.K. started taking part in all competitions and won gold medals in all of them, earning the respect and admiration of his opponents… then… His Master, became part of his life and changed him from hate, to admire and respect, wishing to have this Man with the unlimited knowledge in Martial Arts and Human Behavior; to be his natural Father he never had. >

When finally comes to his senses and realizes of what just happened. He then mobilizes all his strength and asks his Mother to forgive him, as he will explain to her about his reaction, but after she finishes her story.

His Mother decided (after looking at Persa first) to tell him more about her child's Father:

"Well G.K., while I was waiting in vain for my fiancé to write me a letter, or to send me a ticket, telling me to go to join him, I went to have my third examination and Scan at the Gynecologist, as I was 7 months pregnant."

She takes a breather and carries on:

"To my pleasant surprise, I heard the news that my child was healthy and a boy, which my fiancé always wanted to have. Few days later though, I received a phone - call from the Doctor telling me that I had some health problems, which could be of a danger to myself, but I had to wait until the birth of my child first to have a clear view and give me medicines or perform an operation if need it. After that, I had to go through further tests. I had so much joy for the coming of my boy that I didn't care about me at all." She carries on after wiping her tears again.

"I had a normal birth, but the doctors kept me in Hospital and did some more tests. They told me that the results would take some time, and they send me home. To make the story short, after 10 months of coming and going to Hospital, the Doctors told me that I had a rare type of Cancer in my brain and I needed to go to the USA as soon as possible…"

She drinks some of the mineral water and carries on:

"Out of all the troubles that I had; without any news of the Father of my child, which I named him also Giorgo (George), although I hated him, but he resembles him so much… then, some good news came out of my only Aunt who was an American - Greek, living in Boston. I phoned Aunty Elena and told her of my ordeal. In two days time a travel Agent in Athens call to tell me that I was leaving for Boston on Saturday morning. I was desperate that time, as I was very young, only 20 years old. I left for Boston and I gave my Son to my Cousin and her Husband to look after him, as they had no children of their own. Unfortunately, after 10 months, they both killed themselves in an accident, after coming back from a wedding, and I new nothing about it. The few relatives that they had, decided to send my Son to the only orphanage in Athens, as they thought I was lost in the USA, and some day, if I come back… Thanks to my

Aunt, they didn't give my child for abortion, as she was sending money to my cousin, until the draft came back to USA. When she investigated the matter without telling me anything, she found out that my Son was in the orphanage. She calls them and organized to support them in order to keep my Son there and look after him until further notice. She couldn't bring him to USA because he was of unknown Father and if exposed to the Welfare, they could give him for adoption"

"So how old was your child when you left for USA?" G.K. interrupts her.

"He was only 10 months old, just started talking, he was so sweet…"

"But you said earlier that the last time you saw him was 10 years old." G.K. said interrupting her again, because he never remembered anybody to come and see him while he was at the Orphanage, let alone his own Mother.

His Mother tried to explain to him but she becomes dizzy and she wasn't feeling well.

G.K. told her to finish their conversation after breakfast or later on… They all agreed.

## CHAPTER TWELVE

We see them coming out of a rented car, walking uphill towards the temple of Aphea.

They pass the gate where Mrs. K. pays for the three of them at the kiosk. G.K. buys a book about the Historical part of the Temple giving it to Persa and while Persa buys 6 Cart Postal, giving 2 to her Mother and 2 to G.K...

They started walking slowly admiring the Ancient works of Art that has been built 2500 ago. Some of it has been destroyed from earthquakes. Some times they look through the book discussing every detail of it, trying to find out more about the Temple.

Persa takes some shots with her camera.

G.K... felt like something or somebody directed his feet towards the Temple... Without hearing he own voice, he whispers something to his Mother and Sister. Something like: "Not to get shocked"

At this times inside the area of the Temple they were only the three of them by themselves and nobody else around; G.K. takes his shirt and his jean trousers off, unveiling a body that reminds of something between a Boxer (his upper body) and a professional Soccer player (his masculine legs).

He then, tells Persa to be ready, as he will get to the top of the Temple and she can take a shot while he will execute a little difficult sidekick, in honor of the Ancient Olympic Pagratiates.

In few seconds he was on the highest part of the half ruined Temple.

He lifts his right leg and stretches out, with half of his body out in the open. While he holds it stretched out, he tells Persa to take a shot.

The girl is astonished of what she sees, but managed to take the shot.

His Mother cannot believe her eyes, but never the less she begs him to bring his leg back and come down.

G.K. comes down like a cat without disturbing the Ancient Temple. He gets dressed quickly.

After a while and after they have seen it all, decided to leave and visit the Church of Agios (Saint) Nectarios where is nearby.

They are getting into the car with G.K. on the wheel, but again nobody sees another car (also rented) with three foreign men in side (Albanians) following them.

The new church of Agios Nectarios (the old church as well) was built at a pictures hillside, providing plenty of parking for its pilgrims.

Inside the Church, the Pilgrims will have the pleaser of touching to tomb where the Saint Nectarios is resting. So much they believe, where almost all the people after touching the tomb, they listen as well, hoping to hear the Saint moving inside his tomb, thus, will bring them health and prosperity, even cure them from a non curable illness. After they paid their respects to the Saint, Mrs. K. left a piece of jewelry (a gold ring) as a gift (Tama) for the Saint to help her finding her Son!

Please note: The Author when was writing this Fiction Story, never thought of advertising the Saint and his wonders or the Island and its Ancient History. But where ever you go in Greece, there will always be some Historical parts (As the Mount Olympus) to experience, thus, makes it very exited and more interested to the visitors and to the tourists.

They are now coming down the stairs and before they are entering their car, they decided to go across the road to the Curios Shop and buy some souvenirs while they had some cool drinks as well.

They are all seated on the under cover terrace, ordering cool drinks to the old Gentleman. He looks like he is the proprietor.G.K. noticed in the car park earlier; there was another rented car besides theirs, but he did not see the people at the Church or around the area.

As this time of the year is the beginning of the summer season, there were only few visitors during the week.

He took a good look at the car and inside his mind, stored all futures and its registration number.

"Just in case," he talked to himself.

As soon as they took their seats, G.K. gets alert, telling his sister that something is wrong and... before even finished his sentence, three men covered their faces with balaclava (Hood - Mask), are coming from the side of the shop, with the one who looks to be their leader going to G.K. with a gun in his right arm, pointing at his head.

The second one, is holding the old Man with an arm lock from behind, pressing his carotid artery with his other arm, making it difficult for him to breath.

The third is going and grab the bag from Mrs. K.... atleast he is trying to take it, but unfortunately for him, G.K. had a deferent idea than his.

His Mother is sitting at his left and his sister at his right, thus forming a triangle with him in the center. The one with a gun is pointing at his left side of his head.

When the thug is stretching his right hand and touches the bag, then G.K. strikes so fast that nobody of the two thugs closed to him realized what heats them:

He moves his right arm and grabs the arm that tries to snatch the bag and pull it towards the table. The bag snatcher swears in side his teeth (something in Albanian), where at the same time G.K. gets up and drives his right knee to his solar -plexus of the owner of that nasty arm who wanted to steal his mother's bag. Simultaneously with his left arm moves the gun away (with inside-out block) and grabbing it.

Before grabbing the gun, the leader of the gung manages to pull the trigger shooting a single bullet on to ceiling, while G.K. takes the gun a way from him, in a manner, that breaks the thug's index finger.

Before he screams with great pain G.K. with a loud sound, strikes him to the left side of his neck with his right open palm (In side his mind the strike to the neck was for his Mother) while was holding the gun with his left hand. Before the man dropped on the ground unconscious, G.K. with a quick order of his brain, transfers the gun to his right hand.

He turns now to the third one where he holds the old man and tells him in Greek:

"If you leave the old man alone, you can walk a way unharmed, other wise I will blow your dry head off!"

While saying that, he points his gun at a painted picture on the wall where a Dragon has been drawn by a very good Artist telling him to look at the left eye. Without even aiming, he shoots and makes a hole in the left eye of the Dragon.

After that, G.K. turns the gun slowly to the thug, aiming at his head, hoping that he will be scared, as G.K. will never shoot, at least he will not shoot to kill at his face or his body anyway.

The thug, without a second thought, he drops the old man who falls on the ground and runs out of the shop, leaving the other two unconchious on the floor.

G.K. follows him slowly and sees him getting into the rented car and drives a way. He comes in and put his arm around the shoulder of the old man, where with the help of Artemis, managed to get up:"It's over now!"

G.K. also tells the shocked but in reasonable good shape old man to call the Police, giving him his mobile phone.

The old man tells G.K. the phone number of the local Police, but begs him to do it by himself, as he isn't in a good condition right now.

G.K. phones and tells the officer in charge to come to Agios Nectarios kiosk and at the same time to arrest an Albanian who drives a rented car with the registration number ZZA 1522 convertible, Japanese make …

Two hours later

We see G.K. coming out of the Police Station, getting in the car where the two women were waited for him and drives away.

Inside the car he looks at his watch and tells his Mother if they feel to go to eat, as the time was almost two o'clock.

Although tired but satisfied of the outcome Mrs. K. aggress with him, so does Persa.

Not far away is the same Restaurant where they had breakfast in the morning with all the `trimmings` that came with, but all of them, barely had touched their food.

After selecting a table under shadow, as the Sun was very hot, Persa asks her Mother if she could swim over here before eating, as she is wearing her swimming costume.

At her Mothers nodded motion she gets up and takes her shorts, blouse and sandals off, exposing a magnificent body with out an ounce of access of fat. Without hesitation she enters the sandy clean blue water. She stops and turns her face towards G.K. and asks him to join her. "Not to - day Persa, but I promise you next time I will!"

Persa lifts her thump up and dives in the water.

Mother and Son again are at the same place, seated next to each other again facing the sea, with out their glasses on.

The waiter, who is the same one since this morning, greets them politely. He looks at Mrs. K. with a question in his eyes about her health. She understands his expression and she tells him that she is fine; but she will be much better if he brings her a lobster with green salad and mineral water! The waiter thanks her and turns to G.K. where he tells him to bring him Mousaka and salad… as he had much of shellfish the other night at his friend Dimities restaurant with the two girls…

Mrs. K. tells the waiter that her daughter will eat later.

While the man goes to execute the order, she turns her head and starts talking to G.K. with Motherhood voice:

"You know G.K., Persa is a very good scholar and a Black Belt Karateka. She practices regularly since she was 6 years old; has many trophies from competition in KATA and Kumite" (as we mentioned earlier, KATA is a formal Exercise and Kumite is Free Fight).

She carries on by asking him:

"What about yourself? Where did you learn and how long you have been practicing? Your Martial Arts skill is extraordinary! It's not only the execution of the techniques but also the scientific part of it. Your movement's looks like you have already plant them into your mind, and by switching a button electronically you execute them with the a minimum of movements but with the speed of lightning…"

"Please Lady, G.K. pegs her; instead of talking about my skills, let's talk about your Son. My question this morning was…"

"Yes! I remember your question!"

She looks direct into his eyes, trying unsuccessfully to penetrate his will power…

"Well, when I went to Boston to my Aunt, she took me from Hospital to Hospital, from Specialist to Specialist, asking opinions and recommended medicine. All of those Hospitals, used to keep me between 3 to 6 Months. You see, they all new my Aunt how rich she was, as she had 7 hotels all over the States, so they kept me there, experiment on me. The outcome though, was to my benefit. After 6 years, all these experiments directed me to a brilliant Greek – American Brain Specialist, where he said he would cure me by operating me, as I did not have cancer, but a trauma in the brain. My Aunt trusted him and he operated me, making me well and in another 6 months time he become… my husband.

Apart of his profession as a Brain Surgeon, my husband was practicing Martial Arts and had 3 clubs in the Massachusetts area. I never told him about my child's existence, although I am not very proud about it, but I was some how afraid to loose him. After all he saved my life."

She looks at Persa where she was swimming safely closed to the shore and took a deep breath.

"After two years, when my Son was closed to ten years old, I came to Greece with my Husband. When we arrived at the hotel, I told him my first lie that I was going shopping, and I end up in the Orphanage, where my Aunt used to sent a lot of money as a donation, so to look after my Son as well. I beg the Lady call Mrs. Maria to let me see my Son at a distance, when he was playing with the other kids through the open window. She let me inside her office and I saw my Son playing with some other kids. They were playing like they were Martial Artist, attacking him and he was defending himself.

I couldn't resist and I called his name:

"Giorgo" (George).

To my surprise, apart of my son, three other children turned their heads, as their names were also George.

Before I jumped out of the window, Mrs. Maria grabs me with despair, whispering in my ear to stop for the sake of the child...

To my question later on of who teaches the kids Martial Arts, the Lady told me that many times my Son rented Martial Art movies and he himself was more carried a way than the other kids.

"Apart of been a nature acrobat, he is very bright as well, and he speaks English, Italian and French, because you paid for his lessons and thanks to your donations we built the school in side here, so the children will not have to go outside or end up uneducated."

"The Lady Caretaker - Director of the `House`, said to me in a manner that shook me and brought me back to my senses:"

"Unless you take the child home, you must not let him see you! I cannot understand why you do not take your Son out of here? Why you derive him from his Family, from his home, from his Mother and his Father. For God sakes with so much money and you left this beautiful child in an orphanage? If it was for me I would of write to you in USA and tell you to stop sending us money and come and take your Son because I am going to adopt him! Look at him! You think he is happy because he plays and laughs? I know how many times he cried in my arms, asking me where are my Mother and Father, where are my relatives? Do I have Brothers and Sisters?"

&lt;G.K. remembered all of those wards and much more. Also remembers many years ago of somebody calling his name from the window of Mrs. Maria, but in that day, in his group, were another 4 children with the same name as his&gt;

"After this shocking experience, I went back to the Hotel to tell my Husband about my child, but I find at the reception a message to phone the Attorney of my Aunt in Boston, as soon as possible. I phoned him from the reception, to learn that my Aunt had died suddenly in one of her Hotels in Canada. Without telling anything to my husband about my child we took the first available flight back to Boston."

Artemis takes a deep breath and carries on:

"Anyway, my Aunt left me everything. All her wealth she possesses including 7 Hotels and number of valuable properties, also her magnificent Farm."

Mrs. K. wipes her tears:

"Until I took care of all the businesses and assets, visiting all the Hotels one by one, took care of all the irregularities, somehow managed to putt them in order, but took me about 12 months. It was then when I told my husband about my child.

He took me into his arms and instead of giving me hell, even divorce me, he said:

"What on earth you are doing all those years? You left your child in an orphanage? Phone now the Travel Agent and go and fetch your Son! After all, he has no Father!"

"I phoned the Greek Agent in Boston and after few minutes he phoned me back to tell me that in two days time I was leaving for Athens. I did not sleep that night until two o clock in the morning, as you know Greece is 7 hours a head, to call Mrs. Maria that I will go and fetch my Son; only to learn from the staff of the orphanage that they just left for the week - end to visit Mount Olympus.

The day I called was Saturday morning 9 am Greek time, and the date was 15th of July 1983.

As I couldn't sleep, early in the morning I went shopping and packed a suitcase full of cloths and shoes for my Son. I took a quick flight to Montreal Canada to visit one Hotel, not for a specific reason but just to be occupied, as I was so excited and could not wait to go to the airport the next morning."

She wet her dry lips with her tang and curried on:

"Unfortunately God was punishing me! As I was flying back to Boston, my Husband called me in the Airplane to tell me that he will be waiting for me at the airport?

I always phone one of my drivers of the Hotel in Boston to fetch me from the airport, so, I didn't worried this time as my husband would be there, but when I saw his face, then I realized that something very serious had happened!

He told me in plain words, that my Son got lost on the Mount Olympus..."

Quickly she wipes off her tears and carries on, while G.K. looks and listens at her with mixed feelings.


"Since then, I blame myself that I left it that long! Out of all the tears and unhappiness, my husband came to the rescue. This was of what he thought best; he told me that my health was restored and we could have children if I wish. Well, 16 years ago Persa was born, giving me joy but not pain relief as my love for my Son was and always be just as much and more. The other punishment God gave me, was to loose my Husband in an Airplane crash - accident when Persa was 9 years old."

"Do you like to carry on, after we finish eating?" G.K. interrupts his Mother, trying to give her some time to recover a little…
"No!" "No!" said Artemis. "I am O.K."
She tells Persa to come out of the water and carries on, turning her eyes once more towards G.K.
"As much as I could, I took care of his 3 clubs, just for Persa and for me to practice, as he had very good Instructors where they wanted to carry on to honor their Teacher. Still, we are practicing every day, five days a weak. I made my business in that way, so, most of the time I am in Boston and close to my child as well. The only way for me to be able to sleep at night is when I get very tired, and the gym is very good `helper`, otherwise I cannot sleep!"
Although she is tired; while looking at him, something came into her mind:
"Oh! I forgot to tell you G.K. that my fiancé was already a Black Belt in Karate from his years of study in England. Under his instruction, I realized later on in the States how good he was. He was born to be a Teacher. Also as a fighter, I saw him taking part in competition in England and won all his fights, capturing a gold medal at the `All U.K. Universities`. He was very good. I wish he had carried on…"

By now Mrs. K. is emotionally exhausted and tears coming out again…
To stop her tears, she tries by giving G.K. a smile and she asks him to forgive her for being carried away…

G.K. `controls` his hand of not touching his Mothers hair again, while he is saying to her:

"Do you remember earlier where you told me about your Fiancé that he was going to South Africa?"

"And you looked like you new him!" His Mother interrupts him.

"I also agree with you Mom!" Said Persa where she was just coming out of the water…and taking a white towel out of her bag she carries on, looking at G.K. with a meaning in her eyes:

"When you heard his name, you looked like you all of a sudden lost all your blood!"

"Yes, O.K., O.K., I know off him…"

G.K. stops them with his hand not to interrupt him and curries on:

"Not only he is still alive, but also he is the Foremost Grand Master of them all. He is still practicing regularly and he teaches in his Farm only his Senior Students where carried on his Art. He has developed an Art similar to Karate, derived it from the Ancient Greek fighting Arts of Pagratio, Boxing and Wrestling, with his own Philosophy and Style. What he did? After intensive research he analyzed in great length the Ancient Fighters, Pethotrives (Junior Gymnasts) and Gymnasts of that Era, taking the Ancient Roots and brings them up to the 20th – 21st Century with his own Techniques and Way…"

"How come and you know so much in detail?" His Mother interrupts him.

She couldn't interrupt him before, as she and her daughter were speechless, listening to him without believing in their ears.

He looks at his Mother for a whole minute with a thought in his mind. Eventually he let it out:

"From the conversation that you and I had earlier, I came to realize that you still love him. Of what I know he must of love you as well! Actually he loves you more than you love him!"

Again he stops her for not to interrupting him:

"For all the years that I know off him through my Master, I learned that he has never been married, because of some reason. Now I can see that... you were the reason!"

"But why he never replied to my letters?"

"If you want, I can take you to my Master where he will tell you more about him. Even more, he will give you his phones, emails etc."

"But where is your Master?" Artemis asks him with a knot in her throat.

With out answering her question, he gets up, takes his mobile phone and goes through to the memo. He presses the connection button and while the phone is ringing, he walks few meters away.

He comes back, with his eyes fixed at his Mother's eyes, analyzing her to that extent that she is ready to faint again:

"My Master is here in Aegina. If you want, we can go and meet him right now!"

"What?" His Mother asks him with her eyes wide open...

Ten minutes Later

The rented car with the three new blood relatives is moving along from 'Faros' Restaurant towards Agia (Santa) Marina, where is about 8 kilometers away. When strolling along the road and while the two women are carried away from the scenery, G.K. is thinking about the conversation he had with his Master over the phone:

"Hello! Hello! G.K. is that you? You know I can sense you! What is the matter, why your pals are over 80? You must be near! You are in the Island! Have you being running or you have news about your Parents? Are you O.K.?"

G.K. finally decided to talk:

"Ooss (Greetings), Shihan (Master)! I am sorry I couldn't answer quicker, but I have a small problem. This time I am not only coming for practice, but I am going to bring you a woman that you will like to meet... She is Greek, from Boston USA... Please do not ask any questions because I do not have the answers. Could I bring her and her daughter to you? We will be there in few minutes."

"Of course you can! I will be waiting for you and your friends, although I am in the Gym practicing and you may have to wait a while. But why you are so much in tension? I have a feeling that you know the answer of their visit but you do not want to reveal it. You want to surprise me, or... on a second thought, what the hell! All your friends are welcome to my home, but I also have something to tell you! It's about you and me. I cross-examined it and I find it to be real, so you also must be prepared for a big surprise! I will explain to you when you come here. Oh, last night Goddess Athena came to my dream and told me that my life will change very soon..."

With those thoughts in his mind, they arrived at the Villa of Master G.K.

The Villa is situated on a hill, overlooking the Aegean Sea.

Please note! From now on, when is necessary we will address G.K. as A6 or George and his Father as Master G.K., the reason is, they both have the same initials.

## CHAPTER THIRTEEN

The car stops at a very large black gate. To G.K.'s satisfaction the gate opens automatically giving no chance to his Mother and Sister to see the drawings of two large yellow emblems in a circle at the left and right side of the gate, depicting on the left hand side of two Karate fighters with the date, 1973, underneath. On the right side, depicts two Ancient Pagration fighters with the date, 648 b. C., also underneath. When the gate is closed; one can see across the black steel metal and on top of the two pictures mentioned above, a sign is written with the letters:

The HOME of SHOTOKOUNTHIGH - PAGRATIO

Going through a white marble road, they stopped in front of a 4 car - garage. Again the galvanized steel door opens automatically but upwards this time, exposing a white color Brand New Grand Cherokee, with South African number plates and a right - hand steering wheel.

This happened almost every year during summer time, for the past ten years when Master G.K. is visiting his Country of birth. He never thought of bringing G.K. with him in Greece. Instead, he used to leave him free of his presence in South Africa to organize his life for his future, meeting some girls and boys, but practicing regular and take care of the clubs there, as in S. Africa is a winter time and all the Dojos (Gyms) are open and practicing daily.

On top of the white stone built house, the Master has naturally also built a magnificent Gym for his daily practice.The Gym is so much well equipped, that if the professional American film Directors new its existence, they would pay any amount to use it for many Martial and Action movies…

Mother and Daughter holding hands and instead of letting G.K. to direct them towards the house are walking towards the flower-fenced walls of the farm size plot. The reason is very simple:

The two women are carried away from the breath taking view of the Aegean Sea and the clean blue sky, with the Sun's rays touching the Sea - water, reflecting them back on to the sky through different directions. Makes you thing the reason of why Greece has so much colorful Ancient History of Wise Men…

When Mother and daughter are almost in ecstasy of the Natures magical ways, G.K. turns his head back towards the top of the house and bows to his Master, as he sees him through a wide window. He is wearing a white top and black bottom Karate uniform. The Master bows to his Student as well and disappears, closing the curtain behind him.

G.K. is so excited that he has a Father this very special man and cannot wait to tell him… but… he didn't `see` his Mother… where she turned her face to look up, like something or somebody forced her to do it. The only thing that she saw was G.K.'s back.

She looks up on the house, trying in vain to see anything that moves through the windows, because the white curtains were carefully drawn. While looking at the house, she cannot help admiring the way it was built…

She tells her daughter to walk to the house as she has some funny feelings about meeting with G.K.'s Master…

The three are walking towards the front door where on the left and right side of the entrance are carved brown and white stones, forming a fountain on each side, with the water shooting at the left and right side, and both are entering to a small river, through a dark wooden bridge further down, ending up in a small Lake, covered with all shorts of water flowers...

G.K. hurries to get there first as he wants to activate the `Robot`, so the door will be open before the visitors are getting close, so they will not have a change to read the sign on top of the heavy chestnut door. As soon as he comes up the three - step terrace, the door opens before even rings the doorbell.

They are all coming inside, while G.K. is standing in front of the door, covering the gold sign...

A voice in English after welcomes them, commands them to take off their shoes and wore slippers.

To their surprise, G.K. smiles and tells them to do the same of what he does:

He moves to the right side of the entrance hall and he removes his shoes. He places them on top of a wooden stool and tells the women to do the same. As soon as all the shoes are next to each other, then, a green spotlight of nowhere lights on top of the stool and a voice in English tells them:

"Please put on your slippers."

G.K. opens the side door of the stool and takes a pair of black slippers, telling them to do the same.

For G.K. the `road` from the entrance hall to the Library, although is about 20 meters away, looks like he is going to run a marathon. The reason is because they have to go through the lounge, and on the white stonewalls are hanging large pictures of his Master in action, where some of them are in fighting or practicing by himself or with some of his black belt students.

He tells them to follow him and praying that the closed curtains will do the miracle and his Mother will not see him.

Near the door of the library his Mother grabs him from his sleeve asking him:

"G.K., is that you in those pictures? Is your Master Greek?"

"Calm down Mrs. K. you can ask him yourself."

The ray at the door makes it opened automatically and some hidden bright lights are switched on.

A6 tells them to seat down, knowing that his Master will hear him.

Just before they all seated on the comfortable armchairs, the voice of Master G.K. breaks the silence:

"Giorgo (George), tell your friends that I will come down in a few minutes. I am dressing up. Juices are coming!"

All of a sudden the atmosphere becomes much tensed. That happened because as soon as Artemis heard the voice of G.K's Master, although in English, she gets up and her eyes are moving left - right looking in despair at G.K. and her daughter.

The color of her face becomes pale. But she takes a deep breath and not only she managed to stay up, but started walking towards the antic desk while her eyes were fixed upon a large portrait of a Mediterranean looking Karate Master, hanged on the wall, behind the desk.

The Master's looks reminds her of somebody she loved very much, thought he was lost…

A noise of somebody using a hair drier is coming from behind her. She turns her face and she sees a Metallic Robot rolling on wheels, holding a tray with 4 lemon and 4 orange juices.

G.K. gets up quickly and tells his Mother to seat down, because the Robot will not move unless all are seated.

She replies to him that she is not thirsty, but G.K. insisted by telling her:

"We all must take at least one glass of juice, otherwise the Robot will swear at us, in 4 different languages!"

"That is correct!" The Robot replied in English.

Out of all three in the library, Persa, by not realizing of what is happening, is enjoining herself to that extent by saying:

"What a service! This kind of hospitality, you cannot even have it in the USA? Hey, Robot! Bring me an orange juice please!"

The Robot turns to its wheels and strolls towards the young girl from Boston. It stops about half a meter a way from her. With a squeaking noise, turns its tray with the orange juice and extents its arms about 20 c/m., telling her in English with its metallic voice:

"There you are dear!"

The Robot while reversing to its wheels talks to the other two:

"Please come and take your juices!"

"Oh boy," said A6 talking to himself and to his Mother.

He gets up and instead of going to its direction, he moves out of the Robots eye site, going close to his Mother, telling her:

"This fanny machine is going to swear at us, any minute now…"

He stops talking as he senses his Master coming and while he is moving towards the Robot, he is asking his Mother of what kind of a juice she prefers; by addressing her with her Family's Surname, hoping he will hear him:

"What do you like Mrs. Karanikos?"

Before she answers, the door next to the desk opens with out a noise and Master G.K. appears, dressing in an oriental outfit. He directs himself to his student, where G.K. bows to him.

The Master was going to embrace him, but he didn't do it, because he noticed that his student was looking at the one of the two Ladies, who appeared to be the older one.

By instinct, the Master also turned his head at the young girl, while at the same time was talking to his student:

"Giorgo (George), don't tell me that you find your Mother?"

The Master by telling that, he moves towards Artemis where she is already up as she has recognized him...

"But wait a minute!" The Master talking to his student, while at the same time his eyes are analyzing Artemis where she is ready to... drop.

"You told me over the phone that you have no answer of whom this beautiful woman from Boston really is? I have a feeling that for a first time you are not telling... me... the truth!"

He comes as close as possible to Artemis but he cannot find out who she really is. He turns to his student... to find a smile of happiness.

He turns his face again to this well built mature Lady, ready to find the answers from her.

Her voice in Greek, sounds like a thunder inside his brain, making him to be as much as a happy and as much as angry, as ever was in his entire life.

"So, you do not recognize me Giorgo? Am I getting that old?"

The Master of Martial Arts, the Man of no fear, felt all of a sudden the need of stop breathing, and so, he did! By this way, although tensed, his senses were functioning to their limits.

Still not breathing, he comes closed, so closed that both their faces were at kissing distance, and yet nobody does the first move!

But this man is not an ordinary human. In seconds, he orders his senses to overpower his fears and anxiety, by alerting the right side of his brain (the logical side) thus; he felt that the voice he just heard could be of...

"Artemis, is that you?"

He says that in English and he grabs her from her shoulders, not to kiss or at least to embrace her, but to turn her face towards his desk. He then talks to his Robot in English:

"SKT, spotlight"

The Robot almost dropped the glasses as it activates quickly its mechanism and a spotlight from the ceiling hits both their faces, in a manner that it does not reflect their eyes; but never the less, makes A6 to worry about his Parents, as they are both angry to each other for no apparent reason. He takes a deep breath as his mind went few years back where he find his Master holding a picture of a very young woman and tears of pain were coming out of his eyes...

Master G.K. is shaking his head when he tells her:

"Yes! You are all right! You haven't changed much. In fact, time has been very generous to you and of what I can see you have a beautiful Daughter. I don't see your husband around though, which means, either that he is dead or you are divorced, nothing unusual in our days. But what on earth you are doing with my student?"

Artemis tries to stop A6 of not to interfere in this matter and pegs the only man that ever loved, to seat down, as she is getting dizzy.

A6 and Persa knowing the ordeal she had being through earlier are moving to help her because she is fainting.

But next to her, there is a man that his reflexes are faster than anybodies brain. He grabs her in his right arm and he shakes her, while with his other arm grabbing her hair gently from behind, thus, with the sudden shock he revives her before faints and by holding her hair keeps her neck straight of not be damaged by the shock.

A6 is already there with an armchair.

The Master looks at Artemis where now she had placed her arms around him with her mouth to inhale his breath; looking strait into his eyes…

He takes a deep breath, also inhaling her breath, but also, he finds a great relieve of 33 years of pain that inside her eyes, there is a woman in love.

He helps her to seat on the armchair and before he can do or say anything his student is already behind his Master with another armchair telling him politely to seat next to her.

"SKT, water"

"Oss! Shihan" the Robot replies and moves towards its Creator.

While strolling, opens a door upward that is in front of its body and contracts inside the tray with the juices left on it. When closing the door, then at the same time opens another from its left side and a saucer with an empty glass appears.

The Robot stops in front of the armchair of the Master. It lifts its left metallic arm and directs it on top of the glass, purring clear - clean water in it. While the water was running, few colored lights were activated from its metallic head, showing satisfaction of serving its Master.

Before the tray comes to his way, Master G.K. takes the glass.

He thanks his servant and offered it to Artemis.

She takes the glass and after she drank some of it, placed it on top of the coffee table next to her.

The Robot, by moving backwards thanks it's Master and brings back again the tray of the juices in front of its metallic body.

Few minutes later

Now, seating next to each other, holding hands after 33 years of separation, but still, they do not have clear answers yet.

Artemis feels much better now and begs him to let her explain to him first:

"Please Giorgo, I know it will be difficult for you but try not to interrupt me until I finish. If you fill to kill me after I tell you the side of my story, then please do so; as I am already dead!"

With many questions inside his head, the Master decides to wait, at least for the time being, but will his left side brain (the non logical one) wait patiently?

"When you left for Africa and we exchanged vows of faithfulness and forever love to each other, I kept a secret from you. I did it only to test your love for me. What a mistake I made. You never wrote me a letter and...

"What? I wrote you over 25 letters! You never wrote back! In the first five I was telling you that my life changed completely and I went to the Congo instead of South Africa, but you must get ready, as any time I will return there and send you a ticket, to come... to start a family, with many children, all to be Martial Artists..."

"Oh, no," Artemis almost screams. She extents her arms around his neck again and with tears once more in her eyes, brings her face that close with intention to kiss him in his mouth, but thinking of what she is going to tell him, she draws back.

That time of stress and pain, Goddess Athena decided to appear for a first time to Master G.K's mind (not to his dreams as she used too).

All of a sudden, the Master gets up, holding his head with both his arms and he looks like he had a stroke.

With a move of his hand, stops Artemis to get up. He turns his face looking at his student and realizes that he understands of what was happening.

A6 is moving his index finger writing on the air the Capital letter `A` that means, Athena.

The Goddess is talking to him in a manner that she is whispering over his ear:

"Now is the right time for you to learn the truth. In this way your life will change. You must let Artemis to tell you her story, but he, who holds the key for your happiness, is your student. He looks at you, now!"

While he seats down apologizing to Artemis, he looks at A6... and both smile.

"Please Artemis, carry on, I am O.K.!"

She wants to ask him of what happened but to his persistent that he will explain to her later on, she continuous:

"Well, the stupid secret that I kept it from you is that I was 3 months pregnant to our son..."

The man of steel, the most dangerous quiet man in the world (as his students addressed him inside their dressing rooms) and one of the most genius brains of the 21st Century... is about to be out of control... But Goddess Athena is coming again into his mind to tell him in Greek:

"Giorgo, calm down! Calm down! Let her finished first! There is no enemy in this room!"

Artemis sees the `fight` that he is doing with himself and waits for the outcome.

"It's O.K. Artemis; please carry on."

Artemis, after a long breather and a lot of effort, tells him the same story as she told A6 earlier.

"Mother" Persa adds up. "You left out the incident where G.K. saved your life…"

"Its O.K. Persa, A6 interrupts her I will explain to my Master of what happened in Aegina this morning…"

As he standing up 3 meters away from his Father, A6 explains with as much detail as possible. He does this for two reasons:

First, for letting his Shihan to take his mind away andalso to make him feel proud for his student…

## CHAPTER FOURTEEN

Artemis waits patiently until G.K. finishes and she grabs his arm once more:

"Thus, on my way to look for our Son, I find you! Last time I saw him was 10 years old and he was looking so much like you... Although I was disappointed and I hated you, as much as I loved you, in the end, I gave him your name with unknown Father. As you can understand he has my surname. Now that I find you, and you could give him your surname, accepting him as your child... he is lost!"

She takes a deep breath as tears are coming out. She bents her head gently on to his arm...

As she finds no response of understanding and compassion, she lifts her head up and looks at him straight in his eyes telling him:

"That's my side of the story! I came to Athens once more to look for our Son. Now you know everything! As for myself, I am satisfied that I find you and that you never abandon me. I humbly apologize of preventing you of your Son..."

She started crying. Touching his hand again, begs him once more to `take` her miserable life, as deliverance.

While Artemis was explaining about her side of the story, telling him about her dead husband as well, for a first time in his life the Man of steel was fighting with two invisible adversaries!

First: The loss of his Son that always wanted to have.

Second: To find out, that his only love, has a daughter.

Right through his fighting career, he had always find ways to beat his opponent, but opponent that could see and analyze him, using his mind and body as a weapon…

He realized now that when his students used to say… that the only person that could harm him, was only he himself…

Suddenly he remembers Goddess Athena's last words, that:

"His student is holding the key for his happiness"

He looks at his student and of what he sees confirms his last thought to be correct… He is still smiling!

Maybe he looks happy for the shake of my love coming to my life after so many years…

The Master, by analyzing all of those thoughts in his mind, gives time to himself to get read off the sentimentality side, thus, now he is in attacking position as always had, which means; never loosing a fight, any kind of fight…

He touches her hair:

"Artemis, I will find our Son even if I have to turn the world upside down!"

"Now is the time!" A6 talks to himself.

Persa heard of what he said, as both are standing up, next to each other.

A6 noticed that, he comes closer to her, whispering in to her right ear:

"How about you had an older brother?"

He tells that and before Persa closes her mouth, he moves towards his Parents.

As he approached them, he bows to his Master:

"Ooss, Shihan!"

The Master looks at his student who comes to him smiling.

"Ooss Giorgo! What is the matter? You look like you are hiding something. Do you have any news for our Son?"

G.K., standing up in front of his parents makes an effort to keep calm. At the same time mobilizes all his knowledge about Psychology:

"Mrs. Karanikos, what was your child's full name?"

He says that but he looks also at his Fathers reaction.

Artemis hesitates few seconds and tells him in Greek: "Giorgos Karanikos!"

G.K. noticed his Father shaking his head...but he isn't shocked!

"Of what I remember, your Son always had around his neck a gold cross with his initials G.K., is that right? Also he had an accident on his left arm in the Orphanage, when he was 9 years old, and the scar that was left from the stitches could be about 10 c/meters long..."

"Yes! Yes!" The desperate Mother said with more tears coming out. "These two you just mentioned could be very helpful to our search!"

While she talks, turns her face to the Father of her child to find support and confidence, but... his face looks exactly like G.K, s (At the Restaurant) when she mentioned the full name of her Fiancé...

But what is happening? She is in pain! She screams...and while screaming, she calls his name..."Giorgo...I love you..."

The Master without knowing or feeling anything, he squeezes her palm, hurting her to that extent, thus, makes her feeling her fingers will break.

To her scream, he stops and apologizes to her, as he couldn't realize of what he was doing, because all the evidence G.K. mentioned earlier, he was remembering all of them to be in his Student that had in front of him now!

The gold cross, with the Greek initials of G.K. behind it!

The long scar that he had in his left arm, looking like a thin line...

"Oh God, is G.K. my lost Son?" He said in side his teeth, looking at A6...

The answer to the puzzle came from the telephone, which started ringing following by activating the Fax.

The fax machine was on the desk next to the computer.

As long as the fax machine was in use, nobody said a word.

When finished, Master G.K. asked Persa politely to fetch the document as she was closed to it.

She walks quickly and tears out the paper, bring it to him.

He thanks her and tells her to stay close to them.

He then takes his glasses out of the pocket of his robe and started reading it, without making any noise... Almost as he finished reading the fax, his mobile phone rings.

With a magicians move, the phone is in his left arm. He brings it to his ear by saying:

"Hello! Speaking... ooss Deon... I am fine!"

While listening to his Endocrinologist (Dr.) Student from South Africa, he is in full control of himself. At the same time he re-reads the fax.

"O.K. Deon, thank you very much. Keep in touch! Yes, yes, very much. You can tell all my students and rival Senseis as well!"

He puts slowly – slowly his glasses into his pocket and disappears his mobile phone through the sleeves of his robe, then turns to his student who follows every little move or grimace his Father - Sensei is making.

He is not surprised as he addresses to him.

"G.K., remember over the phone earlier when I told you that I have a surprise for both of us? Well, the surprises are now 2 and are very very pleasant...First! We have the same type of blood! And Second! You...are...my... Son!"

Mother and Daughter are speechless, but G.K. without any hesitation comes closed to his Parents and dropped to his knees, with his arms open. When these arms are closed tight, the person in them is non other than his Grand Master who always admired and always prayed to God if he had find his Father, to be... even little... like him. Now he has it all...

The same from the man of steel now melts in his Sons arms and tears are coming out of his eyes...

The words in Greek and English where are coming out of these two extraordinary men, are non - concern of us Readers. After all, it's between Father and Son!

Master G.K. pushes gently his Son, but telling him to stay close, he then turning to Artemis:

"Artemis! You have your Daughter and now I have my Son. What do you say? Why don't you and I, getting married like a mature European people we are, and make them Brother and Sister?"

Artemis is the only one here where does not understand that her Son is in front of her.

Moving her head left right, looking at both men eyes, waiting anxiously for some explanation...

"But we are, Brother and Sister already!" Persa shouts like a thunder in her Mothers ears.

G.K. follows up, Persa's thunder, with another of his own, by saying to his Mother:

"Mrs. Karanikos; my name is Giorgos (George)... I am the natural Son of George Karavidas and Artemis Karanikos! I am your lost Son! Here is my cross, and here is the scar of the accident in the Orphanage". G.K. pulls out the cross from his neck and lifts up his sleeve...

Before Artemis realizes of what was happening, a powerful body embraces her and before she has time to breath, then, two well trained arms, with one around her neck and the other around her waist, squashing her...

As she faints once more, manages to say two words:

"My Son"

Before A6 reacts, Master G.K. holds her hair gently and commands his student:

"G.K., hold her neck with your left hand"

With no time A6 moves on top of the right arm of the armchair and secures her neck as his Father told him.

"Now, press and pinch harder than usual at the second vertebra, then press and rub the neck! Her pulses are dropping and we must give her oxygen. She will be O.K. but she is very weak"

After G.K. has done it...and while Artemis gets around, opened her eyes, G.K. moves in front of her again on his knees, getting hold of her hands.

With a sudden move of both her arms, she embraces both of them...

Through burning tears, words are coming out of her, and if one could heard of those words, should be listening of something like this:

"So many years wasted; my lost Son, my only love; why God? Why all the suffering? I will never let anyone take them away from me again..."

"Mom" said Persa standing up in front of them, with her eyes wet, seen the three in each other's arm.

Master G.K. understands Persas request of not to be ignored at this crucial Family reunion. While seated, he turns his head and looks at his Son.

G.K. who understands his Teacher better than a Son understands his Father, moves to the side of the armchair next to his Mother, thus making available space for another person in the family…

The Master then turns his face towards Persa and with a Fatherhood voice, talks to her:

"I heard from your Mother that you had a bad luck of loosing your Father. From what you just see, I loved and lost your Mother, which was, and still my only love through my teens. As for my Son, I had him every day with me for more than 10 years and I didn't know he was my only child. Of what I am trying to tell you is that we all understand somehow your pain. Unfortunately we cannot bring him back! Out of all your grief though, you also had some benefit, as you mentioned earlier…and that is, you have a Brother. Well, I am his Father and you have the same Mother as his, why don't you join us and…"

Before he finishes his words, an agile body flies through the air and lands on top of the bundle, otherwise a very happy family…

Not the epilog, but the beginning

For over 33 years, the family of unhappiness and grief, at last was united, with an extra member, although squashed on two armchairs, but this time their tears are from Happiness and Joy.

The metallic human who is still holding the tray with the glasses on, is the only one where doesn't share their happiness… Is that the only person in the library?

No! Certainly not! This Family is protected! In fact, has been created by a Goddess, non other than Goddess Athena!

The Goddess is in there to give her blessings, her advises, her commands…

A yellow light from nowhere makes the Family of 4 to turn their heads towards the antic office desk.

"Goddess Athena" Says G.K. looking at his Father and gets up in respect of her. Persa is doing the same. Not because she knows what is happening, but because of her Brother is getting up.

"It's about time she appears!" Master G.K. talks loud from his armchair, holding Artemis hand. "She has some explanations to do…"

The Goddess appears next to the office desk.

The yellow light becomes spotlight, lighting her from top to bottom. She appears like walking without her legs touching the velvet - carpeted floor.

The Goddess has now a human face, with out her spear and her helmet. She is wearing Ancient long white gown. She looks Mediterranean, with her long curly chestnut hair, tight up to a Ponytail. She is very beautiful.

She stops walking and turns her face towards the armchairs. Her melodic voice is talking to Master G.K. as she heard him complaining about her actions:

"You do not have to worry any more! You will live many more years to enjoy and see your family to be happy and grow…"

She moves a little… stopping again:

"I, choose you to find your Son and train him for all those years; after successfully for another 10 years passed all the tests from the Ancient Spirits of 10 Olympic

Champions, Gymnasts and Pethotrives. I choose you, for two reasons:

First: Because you are direct Descendant of an Ancient Olympic Champion - Gymnast of the Pagratio.

Second: To Revive the Roots and Philosophy of the Ancient Pagratio, by Creating Your Own Fighting Art, with your Own Philosophy and Techniques, into the 20th – 21st Century.

"Thus," the Goddess continues, "you become the only person in the world whom really created a Modern Fighting Art that can compete with Karate and other Fighting Arts very effectively. Your great effort and skill will be rewarded world wide very soon by your very rivals"

The Goddess, stops talking and examines them one by one, to see if they have any questions…
She carries on talking to Master G.K.:

"Now that you have your Son that always wanted, and the woman you never forgot; you can relax your mind a bit, because adventures are waiting for all of you! So much for you and your Son, as so much as A5 and his Daughter, even Persa will get involved"

Persa, where up to now had her mouth and eyes wide open, asks the Goddess:
"Me? How can I help? I am still going to school!"

"You and Elpitha…will be directed under your Brothers orders…"
The Goddess is pointing out at G.K.'s face, as she is carrying on:

"It's about time that somebody stops the school crime that happens not only in USA, but also in many parts of the World. Your Brother, now A6, will train you and all of you will be trained by the Grand Master who now holds the hand of his love"

The Goddess softens her voice as she talks to Persa's Mother:

"Artemis! You know that your name derives from the Goddess of Hunting, call, Artemis?"

When the socking but otherwise happy mother nodes at her, the Goddess continues:

"I have nothing to do with the letters you never received. The person, who kept them and destroyed them out of jealousy, was your cousin. She will pay for it! Your time though, of looking and running around to find your Son is over! You will naturally get married to the Father of your child, where he is now a magnificent specimen of a Man and an excellent Athlete - Scientist, that has no equal in many fields, which he has being created by his very own Father, your only love. You must practice with them and apart of taking care of their health, you will take part in many cases against crime and terror. Use some of your Hotels for these purposes, as from time to time all of you including the daughter of A5, will have them as your meeting place…"

As no one of them had the 'clear brain' at that time to say or asks anything, the Goddess carries on emphasize every word:

"I! Went to your Aunties dream to bring you to USA and make you, her Heir!

Although I Enlighten Doctor Georgiou to Cure you; no God wrote his destiny. All Humans must realize that very few people are Gods favorite. They, themselves, must find their own destiny; that is why they have brains!

As many times Persa is thinking about her Father, I will appear him into her dreams"

The young Girl from USA, but with Roots from Sfakia of Kriti (Father Side), and from Mani, of Peloponnese(Mothers Side), makes a step towards Goddess Athena, to thank her personally:
"Not even in my wildest dreams I could fantasize myself that I will ever talk to a Goddess! I will never forget your kindness to bring my Father into my dreams to hung him and tell him how much I love and missed him… I promise you that I will always obey my Brothers command; after all I love him already! Can I hug you? I also promise that I will never tell my friends in Boston! In any case they will never believe me!"

The Goddess makes a move like she comes down to earth by an elevator.
As soon as her leather sandals touched the floor, she opens her arms telling Persa to come to her!
The young Girl hesitates for a second. She turns to her Mother and asks her:
"Can I Mom?"
Her Mother, as astonished and ecstatic as she is, can only node to her with a smile!
Persa, runs to the Goddess arms.

End of First Part:

## SECOND PART

On the second part, the Author will take you, among other places, to the Jungle of the Ex-Belgium Congo (now Republique of Congo)...

Dear Reader! Now that the Family, after 33 years of separation and pain, find each other and happily are squashed in an armchair, lets take a break.

Make yourself comfortable, have a snack, or a coffee, because on the second part, the excitement you are going to experience, will not allow you to leave your seat.

As I promised earlier I will unveil to you `some` of Master's G.K.'s private life, mainly in the unfriendly Jungle of Congo.

## CHAPTER FIFTEEN

Going away

George Karavidas (G.K.), with his eyes closed, was relaxing on the comfortable seat inside the Airplane of the Olympic Airways.

He reviewed in his mind the time where said goodbye to the only 2 women ever loved.

His Mother: Who brought him up, along with his 4 older brothers.

From tender age, as his Father passed away when he was 11 months old, he grew up attached to her.

He remembers seen her tired face, when she was preparing his suitcase. She couldn't stop her tears when she gave him her blessings and told him not to forget his Country and his Family...

The other woman; was Artemis:

That girl was the only one who really touched and finally captured his heart, shared his dreams.

He met her in England, when he was in the last year at the University for Mechanical Engineering, with Artemis as a first year Student, doing English Literature.

They were young, but very mature for their ages. That happened because Artemis at the age of 9 had also a tragic loss of both her Parents, forced her to grow up with her Aunty, which was her Mothers sister (a widow), and her cousin. Her cousin Alice, as she was 2 years older than Artemis, made everything possible to make her life miserable. Alice's Mother on the other hand, although loved her, did not make any things better for her Niece, as she always gave in to her spoiled child. If it wasn't for the money she was receiving from America, (Artemis other Aunt of her Fathers side), she would give her to the orphanage for adoption, or send her to America, in Boston...

So much Artemis and George had one thing in common; had the same roots. Both their Roots were coming from Mani, of Peloponnesian, and both were born in Port of Piraeus, which is the main Port of Greece.

He was three years older than her...

The destination was to Johannesburg (JHB) South Africa, through Nairobi of Kenya.

The time from Athens to Nairobi was about 8 hours and 20 minutes, with another 2 hours to JHB.

Without any problem they arrived on schedule in Nairobi, for refueling and food supplies.

The announcer advised the passengers of not leaving their seats.

Very soon though, the temperature inside the plain went up to 40 degrees Celsius, as they weren't using the ventilation system.

G.K. looked outside through the window and noticed some black soldiers fully armed having their backs to the plane.

From mouth to mouth, the passengers learned that because of the apartheid in South Africa, the rebels around the area could attack the airplane, as Kenya was suffering of a civil war, although President Kenyata, made tremendous effort to unite the tribes and made Kenya to be the only prosperous Central African Country.

The passengers started worrying of the delay, counting the minutes of taking off...but all of a sudden, 4 black soldiers came into the plane with oxygen masks covering their faces. To the relieved of the passengers, fortunately they didn't carry guns, but... Spray - Machines, where without any warning started spraying left – right, on top of all the passengers, like they were spraying on trees.

Behind of the soldiers, were another 4 men appeared to be workers, wearing orange outfit, like basketball players.

The Orange workers were holding plastic bugs and started collecting all the things where were inside the little net, behind the seats…

After 2 and ½ hours, the plane touched down at Jan Smuts Airport, in Johannesburg.

Although G.K. had an official invitation from the Ford Motor Company where has its Factory - Plant in Port Elizabeth, had to go through the official way of all the immigrants entering the Country, which means that he had to stay for a few days in a hotel.

G.K. and his group ended up in the center of the City. The hotel was call, `Acropol` and the roads name was Kerk Street (Kerk, in the Afrikaans language, means Church).

The time was just over 1 p.m. and the group after they were directed to their rooms, they were called to come down to the Restaurant for lunch.

At the Restaurant, George tasted Coca Cola for a first time. He and the other boys liked it, making comments that soon Coca Cola will arrive in Athens as well.

The afternoon was free and together with another 2 boys about his age, G.K. decided to go around the city. The Golden City, as JHB was and still is, well known.

`The name Golden City was not given without a reason, as Gold Mines are still in and around it.

When you are inside the airplane, ready to land, and if you are lucky to be at the window seat, then, you will experience something that you will remember it for the rest of your life. You will see down below, among the most modern buildings of Africa, some hills of golden sand, reminding the visitor of the hills of the Sahara Desert (but golden). It's really something completely different from the other Countries or Cities having gold minds, because JHB, apart of being built on a hill, it was also build after the discovery of gold.

In time we will have the opportunity to talk more about it`

As soon as they opened the door to get out of the elevator, they stop in surprise as they saw some broken glasses on the floor and stains of blood. They looked around to find somebody but in vein.

Very tensed, they walked out of the hotel, with everyone making his own thinking. G.K. noticed it and tried to make a jock by saying that could be the waiter was drunk and they fired him…

At the Restaurant, some other immigrants from Germany where were arrived few days earlier, told them about the `Tea Room Bioscopes`, which was another `First` for the young and inexperience lads…

At the second block, they find one of the `all – day` Cinemas, Tea - Room Bioscope. These Cinemas could be found only in JHB. The funny part of it, was when entering the Theater, then, a young girl followed them to their seats and taking their tickets, to come after few minutes with three small glasses of Coca Cola. George looked around and managed to see through the darkness that were some more Coca Cola glasses in front of the audiences seat, All the seats were converted in a way that the tray - like was resting behind the front seats along the passage of all the seats.

Although it was a pleasant surprise to them, they didn't touch even the glass, as they find it to be non hygienic (the truth was that the glasses were very clean and hygienically treated).

At the first interval, G.K. asked his friends if they wanted to come with him out as he was going to find a Karate Gym (Dojo), if it was operating in that area, so to visit and practice the few days they will stay at the hotel. He always had his Gi (Karate Uniform) with him. In fact, the first cloths his Mother put in his suitcase was his Gi and his Black Belt.

His friends told him that they would stay on, because apart of the Cow - Boy film they would see; also they noticed three blond girls looking at them, so, they will try to make friends with them, although their English weren't that good.

G.K, between Karate and cheating to his fiancé, he chooses Karate and politely told his friends, that after the show when they will meet them later at the hotel, he can help them in English if need it…

`The air in Johannesburg smells peculiar and if you are a visitor from another Country you will certainly complain to the health department of the Municipality. As for the people of South Africa, not only they do not complain about it, but they are very happy and proud instead. The reason is, that around sixties, the Scientists of this magnificent Country, managed to convert coal (where is plenty in the Country) to produce industrial crude oil, thus, the Sasolburg 1 was created with Sasolburg 2 to follow, pending for Sasolburg 3, which could cover 80 % of the Countries energy, making South Africa independent to oil`

Although they spoke English, he noticed that in the hotel, all the waiters spoke Afrikaans (a mixture between Dutch and German).

G.K. for not getting lost, he walked to the next parallel street, called Prichard.

After two blocks further down, he noticed with a pleasant surprise of a Book Store, with the Letters: Hellenic Book Store.

Without any hesitation he walked in the shop. He introduced himself and there he learned that he could get Greek newspapers and magazines. To his question if they new a Karate Gym (Dojo) in the area, they open a telephone directory and gave him few addresses with their telephone numbers. He stayed there for over an hour and a half. He left with a promise to visit them again and will be a subscriber for a weekly newspaper, regardless the City he will end up working.

He arrived at the hotel just in time for dinner. While eating with his friends where they also had arrived few minutes earlier, they told him about their experience with the three girls. In fact, they will meet them outside of the Tearoom cinema:

"Tomorrow at 7 p.m." said Dimitris. "Please George come with us to help us with the language…"

George, although had no interest to get involved with another girl, he promised to help them:

"I will help you guys with the language, but my mind and my heart is back in Athens to my Fiancé, where I promised her to be faithful and as soon as I will settle, I will send her an invitation to come here to get married… You know that she has no parents and she will feel very lonely. She is in my mind and my heart all the time."

All of a sudden the atmosphere become tense, as G.K. was very serious. Both his friends not only agreed with him but also admire and praised him instead, for having the will power to be loyal…

Suddenly from the entrance of the Restaurant, four men appeared.

The three friends stopped talking and turned their heads in surprise.

The four men were well dressed, and had funny short military haircut. They tried hard of not to be recognized as police or military officers.

Each one of them was carrying under their armpit a file with some documents in it.

They spread around by going from table to table talking to the young and inexperience immigrants, saw them some documents...

The Restaurant itself was over two hundred square meters in size (over 600 sq feet), and at that time was full of young immigrants where were they had just arrived, with some of them the previews day.

The man, who approached G.K's table, had a Soldier - Major look, with his mustache going across from his left side to the right side of his sunburns.

"Good evening Gentlemen! My name is Van Royen and I am a Captain in the Army of the ex Belgian Congo..."

G.K. surprises the man by stopping him with sharp tongue and good English:

"Why are you coming to us? What do you want from us immigrants where we just arrived in this Country?" Said G.K. as his eyes were penetrating the big Dutchman, where he was far away of a Captain in the Congolese Army, but born and bread in South Africa.

Surprisingly, Van Royen was prepared for this reaction and especially from G.K., as he appeared to know a lot about him, thus before he answers, he pretended to look through the documents to find his file, where Georges file was right on top of the bundle.

During the time when Van was searching, G.K. couldn't help himself to analyze him:

`This man could be lying or executes orders from somebody else above him! Even more, they paid him to recruit inexperience immigrants`

Van Royen finally lifts the file and started reading it:
"Your name is George Karavidas..."

After finished, he closed the file and carried on talking to G.K. where he was astonished by the information this man had, but most of all he was surprised of the pronunciation of his surname. The man new him very well!

"As you see George", Van carried on. "We know everything about you, even your excellent achievements in Karate, but we are only interested in your Technical capacity of Auto Mechanical Engineer, because the Belgium Conquerors when they left the Country in a hurry, abandoned hundreds of cars and machinery after partly damaged them. They damaged mainly the Engines and the Front Suspensions. We need you to repair them and give them to the Army and to the Officers. Please read all the documents that I am leaving with you and your friends. The interested parties can respond up to five days time, at the address below. If you come, then you must dress up with a suit and tie. Bring your passport with you and your personal belongings. Although you will be given everything there, including of course, your military outfit. Very soon, you will be promoted to an Officer..."

Van, without saying goodbye, drops three documents on the table and turned his back to them, started walking like a Soldier towards the door where his comrades were waiting for him. They all left in a hurry.

<In our lives, most of us, could be we, are making our dreams and writing our destiny, but with the likes of Van Royen and his bunch of criminals, will turn all our dreams to a nightmare and if we managed to survive and get a change to tell our children about our experience,

then, other that we are very lucky, or we had the power to resist and learned from it instead.

When we are young though, our blood boils for adventure, and we do not take advice from nobody, as we know everything… thus, we becoming impossible...

In the contract, they were promising the world (regarding money), making the young immigrants to think of becoming reach much quicker of what they were dreaming when they left their Country of birth, looking for a better future in South Africa>

## CHAPTER SIXTEEN

Five days later

We read from G.K.'s dairy, MY LIFE IN AFRICA (which is still saved up to this day):

In the contract, everything was exaggerating...

I will write only two clauses (if you call them clauses):

'When you are involved in any kind of battle with the rebels, you will receive 400 pounds a month, and 200 pound a month if you not.'

'When you die in battle, your next of kin (where nobody was notified, because no one of the parents will agree to send their children to die in Africa) will receive compensation of 10 000 pounds...'

We still reading from the dairy

These 5 days, that I had to make up my mind of going or not to the Congo, I went crazy. I find myself imagine of been reach and come back to Athens, opened business and married my sweetheart.

During the first night though, at the hotel, after the visit of Van Royen and his bunch, I went to bed with a lot of questions in my mind. In my sleep, I dreamed again of Goddess Athena, where comes most of the nights since my Karate fighting days in England.

When I saw Goddess Athena for a first time 3 years ago, was after my first tournament where I used some unorthodox fighting(Inside the fighting rules of course) techniques to win my first gold medal.

She was at a distance, I could not see her face and I could not hear her voice, but she was pointing at the horizon, without a specific destination.

Just before she was leaving, I could listen clearly when she was telling me the Ancient Greek Proverb where in English will read as follows: `

"No one can escape Destiny."

The following night, the Goddess came to my dream again, but this time she came closed and she wasn't alone. Another God, presumably God Aries, accompanied her.

She asked me to look very carefully while Aries (The Ancient God of War) was demonstrating some moves, using his hands and feet.

At first, he moved slow, increasing his speed and power as he was progressing along. The way he was moving and almost all stances he was taking, looked like he was demonstrating Karate movements. I wake up and got out of bad, because his `Techniques` he was sawing to Goddess Athena were my own creation at the time of my fights…

In this manner, Goddess Athena came again over and over, some times alone telling me to follow my destiny, and some times with God Aries, demonstrating my own techniques, thus made me to get out of bed and do them hundreds of times, so I will never forget them. But I did something better; I wrote most of them down as well, practice them again every day, over and over.

The same happened at the hotel; at first, Goddess was talking to Aries from distance, then, like in a movie, Aries started doing some of my techniques that I never had written them down. I wok up and started writing them down, all the techniques one by one before I worm up; and… in the middle of the night, I practiced them over and over. I must of have being carried on for some time, as some people from the next room were knocking on the wall. I didn't stop though and I carried on with out making noises but with more accuracy and with perfection, for at least another two ours.

After the two hours pasted, then, something else came into my mind; I started defending to my own fighting attacks, with retaliation. The retaliation was with the rules and regulations first, and with the rules of no rules after; which means street fight that can save lives...

So, now that I am writing these words, I accepted long mustache Vans offer and I am at the `Kamina Base` in the ex Belgium Congo, rescuing my life for few pounds more of what I would of take if I had stayed in Johannesburg and accepted my position as Mechanical Engineer.

This moment that I am writing into my dairy, I am inside of an empty double story house near the airport of `Kamina Base` of ex Belgium Congo.

Reminds me when I used to see in the Cinema back in my home in Athens, that commando invaded a village in the Jungle... The only deferent's was that we were real and... not only with a small change of surviving from the rebels who were all over, but from malaria as well.

The village consisted of 65 houses where abandon in a hurry by the Belgium Army.

All the houses were having hot water.

At the ground floor where the lounge - dinning room and kitchen suppose to be, there were scattered 3 single beds with mattress on them, with out any linen and blankets, with out pillows as well. No utensils in the kitchen, but the house appeared well maintained and fairly new.

Apart of myself, there were another two Greeks older than me and three Italians between the ages of 30 to 40 years old.

In the `Kamina` area, apart of Greeks and Italians were, Germans, English, Belgians and some South Africans.

Now we went to the huge Restaurant where there was no water to drink, but only beer.

After eating the stake and salad and I was ready to give in for a beer, then, I saw other side across the tables at the officers section, somebody with a pilots uniform, drinking something like orange juice. I got up and as I was with the suit and tie, I walk across and I stop at the table of the officer who appeared to be genuine Belgian fighting pilot. He had Captains rank.

I introduced myself in English and asked him politely if the drink he had in front of him was an orange juice?

"Yes it is!" He replied in fairly good English.

"Could you tell me to whom may I speak to, because I do not drink alcohol?"

Without answering, the forty - year - old Captain, gets up and put his hand around my shoulder, asking me in English with French accent, where my table was?

After I saw him the table, he call one black waiter to come to us and asked him in French to bring two bottles of orange to my table and in the future he must do it every time I am in the Restaurant.

With a broad friendly smile he gives me his hand and greets me, where at the same time he introduced himself:

"I am Captain Jean – Michele…"

After I introduced my self as well, I returned to my table with some satisfaction, that at last in this unfriendly and forgotten from God Country, I find a friendly person in the face of Captain Jean - Michele!

`Now that I am writing in my dairy, is a good change to review of how in the end I made up my mind to come to the Congo from Johannesburg:

Through the Hellenic bookstore I find the names of some Greek businessmen in the Johannesburg area and during those five days they gave us to think about it I visited all, leaving the Karate practice for later on.

Most of them had little or no education at all. About sixty percent were coming from Cyprus, where thirty percent were coming from the island of Mytilini and ten percent from all other places of Greece.

All these people, advised me of not to go to the appointment, where was walking distance from the hotel. The result was; not only I didn't listen to them, but also I find myself trapped in the jungle. I have already regretted…`

The next day, in the Hell of Congo

To -day, I woke up in the morning with a funny feeling that something wasn't right about our departure from Johannesburg Jan Smuts Airport, because they snick us from a side gate into a 4 - engine Dakota without stamping our passports…

I took my passport and open it, to see, that unfortunately I was right to worry, as it wasn't stamped, which means that we supposed to be in Johannesburg and if something happened to us in the Congo, all these compensation staff was a dirty trick and nothing else, even the money they promised us could be false…

Looking at myself in front of the mirror, I started arguing with my conciseness, which it said to me angrily:

"You deceive me! What on earth are you doing? Are you calling this trap you are into, an adventure?"

"I didn't run after an adventure, but for the shake of money," I said to it, knowing the answer!

"Although there is not deferent between the two; you think the money will coming to your pocket quick and easy?" My conciseness carries on laughing at me.

"I agree with you that it is not worth the risk!" I said with understanding for a first time since I took this stupid decision.

"I must do something drastic and quick!" I carried on... Then, I grab my passport and I opened the door of my room...

I talk to the two Greeks where they were staying up stars with me, occupying the other two rooms, and we came down stares to talk to the three Italians where they were using the grown floor as sleeping quarters.

Until I convince them to saw me their passports, we had a Greek – Italian argument (Nothing unusual), but when I saw them at their very own passports and explained to them of what we all so stupidly had done, they become my best friends...

"What is our next move?" said Gino who spoke some English.

"We must go and ask them to pay us some South African money up – front, as a deposit. In any case if they pay us or not, we will sign up for returning to South Africa. What do you say?

They all agreed!

Here, at this moment is where a funny thing happened.

They called us by using a funny trumpet, to go as we were, dirty and with our suits, as we had no other clothes to wear on. Of what I new they wanted us to perform some commando exercises...

Thank God, I already had a shower, used my vest as a towel, changing at least my underwear, but I had to use the same white shirt, as I had nothing else to wear.

The idea of the inspection was to meat the Mystery Major where was in charge of the whole operation in the Congo.

Eventually the alarm was false, as the Major didn't come, probably because we didn't have uniform. Anyway, we went to the soccer field, where for a tropical country was so dry, that the entire field had no grass at all.

We were about 120 Men with 4 Soldier Majors.

We formed a human triangle, with one man in frond, two behind, three after, etc.

I will not describe the exercises or the maneuvers we did, as were pathetic, with no meaning of a Soldier in combat…the only thing that worried me was the damaged of my tailor made suit, my shirt and tie, let alone my new leather shoos.

The whole exercise lasted about 30 minutes.

At my question to one of the S/Major of when we will get our gear, he answered me:

"Tomorrow man, tomorrow!"

The man appeared to have no idea about it, as they called us again after an hour to come and get our gear.

In the heat of about 40 Celsius, we offload over two hundred bags from a Dakota that had just arrived.

As I opened my bag in my room, I realized that everything in the bag was from USA.

Later on I will try to write where the guns came from.

In the Congo and general in Africa, the sunset lasts only few minutes, as the night is in a hurry to take over, quicker than any other Continent.

As I mentioned earlier, the other two Greeks and myself we were occupying the first floor, where the three Italians were staying at the ground floor.

As I was looking through my window just before nightfall, I observed that, the entire double story cottages had a small garden and all the houses was very closed to each other, with some of them sharing the same fence.

"Now" I said talking to myself. "How will I describe us men?

Still talking and writing I gave some descriptions that I thought was best for all of us, emphasize every on of them:

"Legendaries", "Adventures", "Conquerors", "Piece - Keepers", "Idiots…"

I think Idiots will be ideal name for us all!

I also noticed with a surprise, that in between of some cottages where were occupied by 5 or 6 men, were some small Huts made by straw and clay, where inside were staying large black families of 7 to 8 people, ignoring the empty modern double story houses with hot water…

To my question, during lunch - time to one of the Soldier - Majors, called Jack, told me smiling:

"The blacks never go into the house because they believe to be evil from the whites where were occupying it."

`As we were going to bed early, because we didn't even have a radio, I find a lot of time to practice for more than two hours a day; not of course the Japanese Karate where I had a black belt, but the techniques I had develop, where Goddess Athena and God Aries were reminding me in my dreams all the time.

After practiced them over and over I started realizing that the Roots and Philosophy were coming direct from the Ancient Pagratio (Look at the back of the book), but the Gods were letting me use my own Philosophy, so, to develop my own techniques in a form of execution, to suit the present rules of competition Karate.

The most exiting part that made me carried on and on, practice with out stopping, was my very own body, it felt that it was molded to execute these techniques, of this unorthodox but very effective Art. The effectiveness weren't only for the competition techniques, but also and more for the combat fight as well`

A noise from downstairs interrupted me. I looked at my watch and the time was 10 p.m.

I opened the door and as I was only with my karate pants and my black belt, I started coming down the stairs…

<Of what I am going to describe, will not be suitable for children under 16 to read it. If they do, then an adult must be with them! >

In the center of the lounge, were two young black girls, about 12 to 14 years of age naked from the waist up and a white skirt opened at the side, exposing their buttocks. One of the three Italians was up and the others were lied down on their beds looking at me, smiling happily…

The Italian who was up, came closed to me and gave a condom, sawing me the girls. Just as I took the condom, the other two Greeks were coming downstairs. They were looking very funny with their long under punts, making the Italians and the three girls to laugh.

The three girls came up to me and they extended their hands to embrace me, as out of all of them I was the youngest and well build. They were talking France. Although they weren't bad at all, they smelled like rotten meat. I must of have pulled my face as I saw the Italians smiling again.

I pushed them gently and I gave the condom to the Greek that was closed to me. His name is also George, about 45 years old, bold, small frame, wearing glasses. He came to South Africa from Belgium. He spoke French.

The other man was fat and appeared to be a professional crook. He was half bold, almost the same age as George. His name is Sofoklis (I will call him Sof) and although he was born in Salonika, came to South Africa from Brazil.

Sof looked at the condom and instead of taking it from George, he grabs one girl trying to take her up stairs.

The girl refused and took my hand instead, talking to me in France, sawing me the stairs.

George told me that she wants me to go to bed with her with no money.

I pulled my hand from her grip and told her in English, that I was married.

Sof was almost mad. He grabs another girl and tells George to tell her, that he will give her 5 dollars.

Although the conversation was in Greek, but the magic word...dollars, was in English, when the girl heard the word dollars, she started running up the stairs, with Sof puffing behind her.

George took the willing third girl upstairs as well. As for the first one, she started running towards the door crying because I refused to go with her.

Before I went upstairs, I asked Gino, who spoke English, why they left the girls to go up and they didn't keep them for themselves. After all, they organized the whole thing.

Instead of answering me, he saw me the dustbin in the corner.

I went and look inside. Of what I saw, was few used condoms, which means that my friends upstairs were now having in their arms, two professional prostitutes.

After about an hour, while I was writing a letter to my fiancé telling her how much I loved her, I heard Sof talking to George in Greek, just out side my door.

"George, tell the girl that I want her all night."

George asked her but she refused, as she had already two children, but they could come tomorrow if they want.

As the girls were walking down the stairs, Sof said to George:

"Hey George, the little George from Athens, he is a pushy, I will have the girl tomorrow…"

Before he finished his words I opened the door and punched him on his face. When he went back, he hit the wall sideways. Before he realizes what hit him I lifted my leg and kicked him with a roundhouse kick to his ribs, with the ball of my bare foot. He fell down unconscious, like a heavy bag.

While he was down, I find myself swearing at him, with words I never used before, even in my worse anger.

George shouted at me that I killed him. He shouted at the Italians who were coming up, to go for a Doctor.

The one must of have going for the Doctor already, as the other two and George embrace me, with Gino telling me in Italian:

"Calma Giorgio, calma!"

It was also a first time in my life that I lost control and took me some time to realize it.

Fortunately the Doctor came alone, as every body else was a sleep. He revived him by opening a capsule and placed it under his nose. Sof took some time to realize of what was happening, but he was in great pain at his left rib side…

If I will ever be blessed to have children, or be culpable of teaching Karate, I will advise them all, when they will be at a similar situation, to use their good and strong character, by politely demanding an apology for whatever been said to them:

"Use your fighting skill, only when you have too, and only when the Law is protecting you"

I wasn't very proud of what I did. The only excuse that I gave to myself that I was only 22 years old.

Into my dairy "In the Jungle of Africa" I will not write the surname of everybody, unless that they will write it by themselves.

Next day

The following day was also very funny, makes me realize once more of my fatal mistake of going to the Congo.

After we all men waited for some time in the heat of the tropical Congo, finally his Majesty Major Fiersen (That is not his really name) appeared with his two Captains as his permanent shadows (If those men were really Captains, I was Father Christmas).

Major Fiersen was the man in charge of the whole operation, but it looked like (Although I do not knowing it yet) he had nothing to do about the recruiting.

We heard rumors about his achievements, but to me he appeared to be not less crook than Sof.

While he was inspecting us, he thought it appropriate to explain to us about our mission:

"We are Commandos," he said (Here we can laugh) and he looked at all the men, like we were the best in Africa.

"We will operate in small groups as our main objective will be Hit and Run."

Now, this `Hit and Run` was again foolish, as in the Country was a Civil War between the Tribes, where in one day one Son of a large family was a Rebel and the other Son was in the Army. The following week they changed places, not because they changed their ideals, but to survive, as the worse enemy of both the Rebels and Tshombe's army, was poverty and hunger.

As he had nothing else to tell us (Such as, of what about money), he started walking away with his two shadows behind him. The Two `Captains` collided with one another and both of them almost hit him as the Major stopped suddenly. It wasn't anything to laugh, but to cry…

He pretended that did not see anything, as he called Soldier-Major, named Jack. He told him something and walked away, again with his two shadows…

Jack turned to us and told us with a loud voice:

"Tomorrow, you will be given new weapons and very soon you will be going to Albertville to free white families as they have been captured by the Rebels."

With this command, he sent us strait to hail with slim chances of surviving, as the Rebels were scattered by thousands all over the Country.

Strait after that, we went with most of the Germans, Italians and some South Africans, to demand money upfront, as they all had seen their passports weren't stamped.

I forgot to write in my diary, that back in Johannesburg, just before left, I opened an account, in case they bank some money for me…

The next day find us with new mashing - guns.

While we were cleaned them up, the 3 Soldier-Majors gave each of us a document to sign. Included was the serial number of the guns as well, but all were written in France.

I asked George to read it. After finished reading it he become very upset, because they were telling us to sign that we voluntarily wanted to go to free the hostages at Albertville.

Another words, although there were no money, they used that kind of sick Psychology to touch our humanitarian side. The result was that few men signed it.

The next day, those signed the document, were called to get ready, as they will go to Albertville. They were about 15 men, mostly Germans.

When they were loading their gear in the Dakota, I went to look, as I felt guilty of not going with them to free the hostages…

Apart of their guns and ammunition, they were loading two funny looking boats, made from fiberglass, with out a keel. To my question about it, Jack told me that they were going to use them to go around Albertville, through the Lake.

"But these boats are not so safe to carry so many men with their ammunitions as well." I insisted to the man in charge.

"What do you care, you are not coming", said one of the Germans, where few minutes ago he was walking with his high black boots, marching like the German Soldiers during the second world war. Also on his left shoulder had stitched the `swastika` (Hitler's emblem).

"It's different to be careless than a brave!" I said those words while I was walking away…

He called my name. I stopped and turned my head, ready for a fight.

"George," he said with his heavy German accent.

"You know? In Albertville, are also some Greek Families being captured there…"

I walked slowly towards him and at about one meter away I said to him in a manner of half serious and half joking:

"You known Hans, although I believe of what you just said and I am going to consider going to Albertville, but as for yourself going along, I suggest you take that swastika off, because you look like a Vulture instead of a Piece - Keeper…"

Next Day

The next day, Sof came from the Doctor where he was going almost twice a day since the night I punched him to the face and kicked him to his ribs; he looked at me and smiled with a relief, but passed me with out saying anything. Later on I learned from George that Sof after going with the girl and with out using condom, he developed Vulnerable Disease and the Doctor had to inject him twice a day for three days.

## CHAPTER SEVENTEEN

Now, I am writing inside a noisy, 2 engine Dakota, going into the mainland of Congo. Apart of the Pilot, no one knows which part of the troubled Country we will land.

Under the shocking eyes of my comrades, where they were all sweating from fear and from the heat, I looked like I was going on vacation or I was a Journalists, with my shirt over my neck, writing into my Diary.

<I forgot to write that while I was at the Hotel in Kerk Street, waiting for the days to pass, I received a phone call from the Immigration that I could go to work at a Service Station, repairing cars, in Florida, which was about 20 kilometers north of Johannesburg...>

But by the looks of it, luck wasn't on my side, but I still wanted to see what God has written up for me...

As for the Dakota, all of a sudden apart of the noise and the heat, started
trembling very seriously.

The Pilot, called Mark to the calk - pit and told him to secure the Jeep properly (We had a Jeep in the Dakota as well).

Mark wasn't the mechanical type and he called me to help him holding a toolbox in his arms.

I tighten some brackets where some bolts were loose. Those brackets were in front and the back of the wheels of the Jeep. I also secured the rails where the Jeep was on them. They were all loose. Most probably the people were using only hands or not proper tools.

I gave the toolbox to Mark. He thanks me and I went back to my Diary.

Inside the Jeep we had all our gear with over a thousand of magazines and ammunitions. The Jeep had no cover and no windscreen.

We were: 3 Greeks, 5 Italians and the South African Captain.

Excluding the Pilot we were 9 brave men going to become Heroes.

Gino, got up and went further down next to the Jeep, to try to get some sleep on top of some plastic containers, while the other 4 Italians were talking loudly about the mafia and what they were going to do when they will come back in Johannesburg.

I asked George, where he was sitting next to me to stop smocking, because we had no proper ventilation.

He looked at me behind his myopic glasses in surprise. He was shocked because telling somebody who smokes 40 to 50 cigarettes per day to stop or quit smocking is like you are taking the water out of the thirsty mans mouth in the desert.

He extinguished his cigarette, but he dug his left hand inside his personal bag next to him and came out with four packets of Lucky Strike, at the same time he pointed his finger at the Jeep telling me:

"There are another 9 packets waiting for me."

This time Mark came to tell us (With out a map) that we had another 5 hours to reach our destination.

I didn't bother to ask him what was the name of our destination, because he didn't knowing it.

When he left to go to seat next to the pilot, I looked at Sof where he was wet from top to the bottom, taking his shirt and vest off, then, using his vest as a towel tried to dry himself starting from his face, looking at me all the time.

"I think he wants to tell me something, I said to George loudly, so Sof could heard my words.

Like I gave him the signal, he got up and comes and seat next to me, in between George and my self. I noticed the 110 - kilogram man was crying.

"Sorry Sof" I said to him with out even thinking...

"No, no," Sof said, "I must apologize for offending you the other night."

He takes my left hand:

"It's my fault, you should kick me before I went up with that whore, not to my ribs but to my balls, so, I could not have the desire to f...the black prostitute."

All the time that Sof was talking to me and crying, he was holding my left hand, while George laughing from the other side, he was holding my right hand (With the pen) afraid that I could punch Sof to his face.

Eventually he released my hand, after he heard me talking to Sof, telling him that was just bad luck, but after the injections he should be completely cured.

<As soon as my `pen` was released I started writing exactly all the words Sof told me, incase I will forget them>

`The two Greeks where were with George in this adventure in the Jungle, were coming from completely deferent background:

Sophocles (as written earlier) age was about 45 years old (110 k.g.), his fat face was not so ugly but his black moustache gave him the looks of a cheep crook, ready to steal, even from his own Mother. He was born in Sallonika, but fifteen years ago he `had` to move to Rio (Brazil), because he couldn't longer live in Greece, as sooner or later he would end up in jail...He was a dropout, barely finished Junior High. He never had a proper job as he never had an occupation or a trade.

When the three met in Kamina, Sof was telling them of his achievements in Rio, doing nothing for a leaving and yet he lived in a luxurious apartment, but the last `trick` didn't work and the authorities kicked him out, ending up in South Africa with papers saying that he was a Plummer.

The other George, was about fifty years old, bold, with myopic glasses and a permanent cigarette in his mouth. He was born in Pireus (The main port of Greece), but very soon his parents moved to Belgium. He had an 8-year-old daughter, staying with his old Mother in Pireus. Both had to rely at his monthly draft, as her pension from her dead husband wasn't enough to cover all the expenses, including the two - roomed apartment. Thus, George the Belgian had to leave Brussels to immigrate in South Africa. The Country of opportunities where those days as long as you had an occupation and a white skin, then, all the doors could be open for you.

Very soon they become closed friends, although they had 25 years deference, but with the young George becoming the adviser of the two; with the bold Belgian to listen to him like he would of listen to his own educated Son`

Reading from the Diary again

Inside the Dakota

`I said to George:
"As soon as we will return to Johannesburg, I will write a letter to my fiancé to start getting ready to come to South Africa. You also must write to your mother and your daughter to do the same. Will you promise?

"If we will come back to Kamina alive, then I promise!"

I looked at Sof and he was sleeping like a baby, letting others to worry about his mischiefs in life. He was holding in his arms his vest and shirt`

`Very soon the two friends also were fallen asleep, but their dreams were completely different to each other.
We will only analyze the dreams of young George (G.K.), as we see it written in the Dairy bellow`

While I was taking a nap in the noisy Dakota, I dreamed about Goddess Athena telling me:

"I do not want you to get involved in a Civil War, but you need to have the experience"

When I tried to talk to her, she disappeared and God Aries came instead, attacking me with his arms and legs, using my own attacking techniques in a manner that I had to use the fighting defensive techniques where I inverted them in my dreams as well, which were; block and retaliate. Another words, the God forced me to practice my own offensive and defensive techniques again and again, over and over!

From the Writer to the Reader:
Earlier, I promised you that the second part would be very tensed and exited. Well, now is the time as you going to do the…

Reading from the Bloody Diary:

As I had no experience (when in the early pages I wrote that I was glad going to the Congo, I was thinking of going for an adventure), now that I have been in the real Hell, now that I had to kill or been killed! Now that twice I escaped death and much, much more…

Only now I have the experience, and only now I realized, that: `Tarzan` and `Jungle Commandos` where we all had seen in the cinema; were only a well prepared Fiction Movies, created by the Directors and their team of the film industry, as the real truth, is far beyond their imagination.

I am writing again into my Diary who survived, but I had to wipe off the blood that was on it. Although the blood it wasn't my blood... I wish it was...
Let's take everything from the beginning!

Before we realized of what happened, we all woke up by a shacking – bumping noise, as we were landing in a small farming airport.
The name of this miniature airport was, Camapini.
We removed all our belongings out of the Dakota. Carefully I reversed the Jeep and parked it further down on the right side, because we were waiting for another airplane to land. We couldn't do some target shooting because it was already dark and the number 2 Dakota was just coming to land.
I run quickly to the Jeep. I started the engine and switch on the lights, before the Dakota landed on top of the trees.
To my surprise, as soon as I switched - on the lights, then all of a sudden, out of no were, fires came from six places on the left and right side of the Camapini airport....
The landing was so funny and dangerous that I will call it, `Jungle – Juggling`
The men helped to off - loud all the equipment and I driven the Jeep out. Park it next to the other. Before I switched the lights off, of the first Jeep, I took a quick look at the back of the second one and I saw some funny machinery. Later on, I learned that it was a Bazooka, with some Rockets.

By now, the time was 7-30 p.m. and the month was July…`

Please note: For Political reasons; the Dates, Years and some names in theStory of this book, will be fictional, but if you follow it closely then you will come as near as the really dates…

`Dear Reader to confirm my note about using fictional names, I only tell you this:

Tonight, December 2004, in Athens Greece, few days before Christmas, where I am reading from the Diary `In the Hell of Congo`, to include some of it into`Devine Justice`, I was watching CNN and I saw another war in the Congo between the tribes, with innocent people been the victims again, but this time wasn't any excuses of foreigners interfering, but their very own people, where they do not have only the survival problem through hunger, but now they have to be refugees in their very own Country, forced them to turn the time back more than two hundred years, by living primitive life in the Jungle again.

I somehow felt a bit better on my conscious, because these so call Rebels of to day and those of the past, have one thing in common: To destroy their very own Country, or better say, they are destroying their very own Families`

Time: 8 p.m. at Camapini Airport

If it wasn't for the six fires, which were still burning up until now, it would of have been completely darkness, as I couldn't dare keep the lights on, incase it could run down the battery, or risking the fuel, if I had to keep the engine running…

I asked Mark what was going to be our next move or if we had any plans. He answered me loudly so all the men could listen;

"We are leaving in 5 minutes."

Before we left, every body finished a beer except me, because I gave half of it to the black guide who would direct us up to a certain point of the Jungle.

Mark asked me to drive the first Jeep and he would be sited next to me.

In the back of the Jeep, we had apart of George the Belgian and Sof, the black guide as well, who was holding the bottle of beer, enjoying every seep of it.

Sof asked me in Greek: "Hey George! Ask him to tell you what the hell is under my feet, they look like pipes."

To my question, Mark answered me, that those pipes were parts of the two Bazookas.

"And where are the other parts?" I asked him.

"At the other Jeep", he said laughing. Thinking that my question was out of proportion I didn't say anything for that, because the man new nothing about military. I wish that we would never loose the other Jeep, because if we had to go to Albertville in different ways, then, the Bazookas would be useless to use…

`The experienced of this adventure, changed me to be more mature and see things completely different, and although I felt I did what I had to do, because, my `enemy` didn't have anything human in him; as far as the Family and the Country was concern. Also, if I didn't have to retaliate, I wouldn't only be dead, but the Rebels would eat most of the parts of my body.

I will right the name of the Rebel - Savages, further down…`

Ten minutes later

Thinking of going to Albertville was easy, but to find the way and eventually to be there was Hell, as the distance was over 800 kilometers on non - existent road as such.

After 30 minutes the black guide left us, keep holding the bottle in both his hands, still some bear in it.

From time to time I will write few sentences about the road, where if had to explain it in detail, then, this Diary would be as small as a scrap pad.

At this moment I will give it a name: The Road to Hell.

After 3 hours of drive, with one Jeep following the others tail, with a complete darkness at the left and right side of the road, we reached a small village with few Huts. Thanks for the two fires burning on the left and right side of the muddy road; we could see few black men waiting for us.

We stop the Jeep and came out to stretch our legs. It was fairly dark and I couldn't see properly their faces, but they were wearing camouflage uniforms, same as us, thus, we could fairly see that they were proper Soldiers.

Mark told me that this place was our first stop, only for refueling.

After this stop, we all felt much better, especially me, because I always analyzed and criticized everything that wasn't well organized. This time I have to admit though, that up to now, things weren't that bad, as far as communications was concern.

Mark told me that he would do the driving, so I could have some rest.

That suggestion couldn't come at a better time as I was exhausted for trying to keep the Jeep on the road, before I pumped to a tree or a bush.

After about 30 minutes we left again:

As Mark was driving the Jeep and I was sitting next to him, I soon realized (We all did) that he wasn't so calm, as he tried to saw us up to now. His moves were spasmodic, like a robot and at every bent or a sharp turn; he strikes the Jeeps left or right rear at everything was in his way. By the looks of it his mouth must of have been dry as he asked me to open a beer for him.

With out thinking, I told him to go to hell! Because according to my rules, drinking and drive was not going together.

He was so surprised that I disobeyed his order where he turned his face towards me to say something.

That split of a second made him to brake, as he hit a very thick bush.

Lucky for all of us it wasn't a tree.

At the impact, Sof went over to Mark's back, hitting his ribs at the parallel bar, swearing in Greek. And George as he was bending forward holding his gun hit it me with his elbow on my right shoulder, where I in turn, hit the dashboard breaking it with my mashing guns barrel.

"Listen Mark" I said furious. "Or go slower, or give me the f… steering!"

At the back, the two Greeks were swearing at him in three languages: Greek, France and Spanish (Brazilian).

"Mark, I know it is very difficult for you to drive a left - hand car, as in South Africa you have used to drive a right hand steering. Try to have the steering always at the left side of the road, and for gods shake, go slower."

He reversed the Jeep with out saying anything.

To my surprise, all my anger helped him, as he was concentrated on the road, but I noticed that his tongue was getting out all the time…

"Please George" said very politely, "will you give me some water from your canteen as mine has beer in it."

"No way" I said smiling, andwith out any other word I opened his canteen that smelled like urine and in front of his eyes, threw all the beer out on the road from the side door.

After making sure that was no beer in the canteen, I told him to stop, as I opened my canteen. After stopping, I pore inside his, half of mine and gave it to him.

"I must say chap!" Mark said with a great satisfaction, after he took down most of the supposed to be water:

"This water you so generous gave me, it tastes like an orange juice.

"Yes Mark it is!" I said to him, understanding the satisfaction of an alcoholic, of not want to drink… water.

"This is the last one, which I brought it from Kamina. From now on we will have to drink water from the jungle, or from our conducts, providing of course, we will use our tablets for Yellow Fever. If you are going to have a beer, then is up to you. But you will drink only if we are stop for the night and not more than one bottle. If you do not value your life, I value my friends and mine."

"George" said the Belgian George, in Greek. "Please tell the Captain that we want you, to drive the Jeep."

I translate it to Mark in English, but before his answer I told him that he was doing fine.

"No! Mark is doing fine" I said in Greek to George, "and I am very tired."

"Thank you Greek, you are born to be a leader", Mark said with out taking his eyes of the road.

Little more about the road to Hell

`Now that I have some time, I will write few word s about the road to Albertville`

Please dear Reader, don't turn the page, it is an experience I wish to share it with you!

This road to be, was about 3 meters width, where in most ways was shorter, with Jungle at the left and right side. If you were the driver or the co-driver and forgot resting your elbow on the open side of the window (No glass was there to close it) for more than two seconds, then automatically you had to bring it back in with a scrim, pain and blood. If you were lucky, then only thorns could come out of the wound with minor scratches (As happened to me 3 times). If you weren't lucky, then some blood with a gush of wound could be expected (Like happened to Mark several times). The worst part was that we didn't have first aid kit...

Under the wheels I felt that I was driving on snow, with loose rocks, sliding at every angle, let alone at a sharp turn.

Thank God, in the end we all arrived safe, but we didn't escape some funny happenings though:

Mark was driving for two hours with out any serious accident. All this time I was holding with my right hand the door at the open window, while my left I had it stretched to grab the parallel bar behind me, chatting to my Greek friends.

Mark tried to understand what we were saying, but was impossible, although in the English language there are over 16 000 Greek words in it!

To make it easier for himself, Mark tried to sing Elvis's song; `Its Now or Never` He was so much out of tune that I had to -stop him with a question:

"Mark!" I shouted, "How long until the next stop?"

Thanks God, he stopped singing and looked at his watch (We all had phosphorous watches, being a present of our gear).

"We suppose to be there in few minutes. We are not much late. Look carefully, to find a Monastery on the right hand side."

To my surprise, we find it in front of us. Mark stopped the Jeep smiling:

"You see Greek? We are here! Just on time."

I shook hands with him and congratulated him. I wish I were wrong about his experience and my judgment...

If it wasn't for its large wooden gate, we could pass the Monastery, as high thick bushes surround it and high trees hide it. Belgian Monks occupied it.

With Georges France, I learned that we were about half way to Albertville and the Monastery was used as a refueling Station and also for the Patriots who were fighting the Rebels.

As I did not see any Soldiers protecting the Station, I asked Mark about it.

"They will come soon!" He said quickly, trying to walk away.

"What about some food?" I curried on.

"They only have food to survive..."

After refueling, we moved again with the other Jeep been in the front. This happened because we took with us a Belgian Officer, where he was waiting for us at the Monastery. His name was Jean.

Mark told me that Jean hated the blacks, regardless the side they were:

"Rebels or Regular Soldiers are all the same for him …"

As Mark was telling me more about the Belgian, he had to strike the brakes suddenly, before he collides with the first Jeep, breaking its tail light lens.

That happens because all of a sudden, the front Jeep stopped and Jean jumped out. The knock did not make much noise…

Jean came to tell us to keep quiet and follow the front Jeep with the lights off. He run and jumps in again.

Although was a full moon, it was impossible for the front Jeep to move with out lights, so the South African driver switch on the park lights. In this way, he helped us to keep our lights off.

I took my mashing gun in my hands, so did the other two at the back. Mark had a pistol at his waist.

Suddenly Sof grabs me from my shoulder and asks me in Greek:

"What's wrong George? Ask him, ask him…"

Before I questioned Mark, he tells Sof to close his mouth and keep his gun ready!

In about three minutes, we arrived in a square, where at the left side of it were three Huts.

Jean who was already out, signal us to come to him. The time was five minutes to one, after midnight.

Jean took Mark few meters away telling him something. Mark came to us and Jean went to his men.

We all instructed by the two `Match stick Heroes` to line up facing the three dark Huts, ready to shoot at them, regardless if there were children or innocent people.

All and all, we were 10 men, going to conquer one part of Congo, where there were (only in that part of the

Country), over a million fanatic Rebels, ready to kill even their own Mother.

As we were looking at the Huts, I was on the right side, having on my left all the men, including the two leaders where were in the center.

All of a sudden, Jean call loud in France, one, two, three and he started shooting with his mashing gun. All the men followed him except me, as I turned my mashing gun on the floor and let three bullets coming out (one by one). After they all finished their magazines, I lifted the gun on the air and finished all 17 bullets where were left inside. Then I pulled the magazine out replaced it with another.

All of us had four magazines (of twenty bullets in the magazine) in our pockets, where some Italian men, had few defensive grenades hanging from their chests.

Every body was looking at me, but although we could see each other through the full moon, I couldn't see their eyes, but I saw clearly the two killers coming at me, with Jean to be in front and the most furious.

He came closed and he grabbed me with his left hand from my chest, lifting his right fist to punch me to my face.

I don't know about the others, if they thought that he was fast, but to me he was very slow, telegraphing his punch.

When he lifted his fist, I moved my right foot back, assuming forward stance, making him loosing balance. At the same time I lifted up the mashing gun, which I was holding it with both my hands, hitting his extended arm, almost breaking it. While the gun was up, I swing it to the left, hitting him on his left jaw with the butt. Although angry, I control the strike, as I didn't want to break his jaw. He went backwards hitting Mark on his way; make them both to fall on the ground.

Mark gets up quickly and directs his hand to his gun.

Although I was positive that I was the only one with the reloaded gun, I gave him no change, as while they were both falling on the ground I followed them.

Before even touched his gun, I kicked him (Behind his left ankle) in a manner of a leg – sweep, as I had done it many times in competition, bare footed. He falls down almost on top of Jean, who was holding both his hands on his swollen cheek. As Mark hit Jean's body with his back, Jean screamed with pain and pushed him to the side. Before Mark realized of what was happening, I slide – jump my right leg on top of his face, stopping it on top of his throat, with out touching it.

I moved my foot back and while I was talking to them I directed my gun to their faces:

"You both are disgusting; you are killing innocent people and order us do the same! Now listen to what I have to say to you: Because we are in the middle of nowhere and because by the looks of it the Huts were empty and nobody was killed; if you both promise me that you will never do this monstrosity any more, only then, you can lead us to Albertville to try to free the hostages."

I carried on more furious:

"Although I cannot see it possible to rescue them, I hope though, that you both have connections or a plan. Is that clear?"

Thank God, when I turn my face towards the men, all agreed with me.

I help Jean to get up and while he was apologizing to me in English with his French accent, I realized that, the arm that supposed to punch me to my face had also been badly damaged. That happened when I lifted the gun up I most probably strike both the arms. As for Mark, he got up dusting himself swearing inside his teeth.

I ask Jack, the driver of the other Jeep, if they had any first aid kit in their Jeep.

"Yes we have! You want me to fetch it?"

When Jack brought the metallic first - aid kit, I called Jean to come to the Jeep who had the park lights on.

I made a sling for his left arm and bandage the wrist of his right, rubbing his jaw also, to put down the swelling part.

With Jean's both arms covered with bandages, we started again in the middle of the night, with Mark on the steering and the two Greeks wondering at the back.

Jean was again in front with Jack driving the Jeep, with us followed at closed range. Both the cars had their lights on.

No more than 10 minutes of drive we stopped at an opening where some of our comrades from Kamina were waiting for us. We did some changes (The order came from the two Heroes) and to my surprise, the new comers where moved into our group, shook hands with me to congratulate me about of what happened earlier...

We moved again with out knowing how far we were from Albertville.

After few hours of hell driving, the night had almost ending its long journey and the sunlight was taking its place when we reached a proper City, but it appeared that a heavy storm or a hurricane had hit it very badly.

We stopped and we were instructed to come out and form two lines on the left and right side of the road, with Mark and Jean leading their groups.

Lucky for Jean, his right arm could be used to fire.

After about 100 meters of walking, Jean lifted his right open palm to signal us to stop.

Without saying anything, he pointed his index finger at me, and at the two Jeep behind us, signals me to go and guard them.

With out a word I started walking back towards the two Jeep, feeling inside my stomach that the order wasn't for me to guide the cars, but to get me away from the group.

From that place I couldn't see them, but I could hear them, because it was so quiet, as there were no people at all, looking like a Ghost - Town.

I heard shoots, first from a pistol, and then from mashing guns, sounded like there was doing target shooting...

I went behind the Jeep with my mashing gun ready.

Suddenly, I saw Gino, one of the Italians, coming down the road towards me. When he came closed I saw him smiling:

"George," he said with his broken English. "Jean wants you there. I stay here!"

I didn't ask him of what they were doing there, because I couldn't understand him.

While I was walking towards them I heard shots again.

When I finally reached the top of the road, I saw the most stupid target - shouting I ever seeing in my life, even from the cowboy movies in the cinema, where they were shooting at tin - cans.

The men were shooting at an empty Hut, where it was built in the middle of the City, most probably as an attraction for the non - existed Tourists...

I heard Jean shouted at the men, telling them in France:

"Shoot the enemy, before he shoots you!"

I could see his eyes; they were looking very angry, ready for revenge...

Mark was telling me earlier in the car, after apologizing to me again, that the Rebels had killed Jean's Parents.

To my question of why he hated all the blacks, he said: "The Rebels or the Regular Army soldiers, as far as Jean was concern, they were all criminals and cannibals"

Mark saw me coming and shouted at me:
"Come on George, let's do some target shouting. There is your target!"

To maintain solidarity between my comrades, where in this unwilling and unpleasant war, I had to be next to them, side by side, as we had to face a common enemy who ever that was. That's why I started shooting, but one by one and on a certain target, which was one of the four wooden poles of the Hut.

The bullets of all the men doing shooting on the poor Hut, made it looking like it were a `Summer Hut. `

After I finished the entire 20 - bullet magazine, I re - loaded slowly – slowly. I also re – load the empty magazine from which I used it at the very first time when I shot on the air, outside of the three empty Huts...

I noticed that the men started doing the same as I did...

Now on my belt I had only 10 bullets left, but I had 80 bullets on 4 magazines...

We left in few minutes.

Twenty minutes had past, when we reached a military camp.

I noticed some small and large Huts were around the camp. I learned later on that some of the large ones were used for quarters of the officers and some for warehouses, save the small ones for the soldiers and the low in rank.

Mark told us not to come out of the Jeep, while Jean although hated all the blacks, had to go to meat the man in charge, because he could speak France.

The Officer in charge was very colorful regarding his uniform. I couldn't see his face properly but through some fires scattered all over, I could see his uniform and some medals on his chest, like he was going on parade…

They only had few minutes of talking. When Jean left him coming to us I saw his hand going for his gun. He turned his head back, but the colorful officer wasn't there…

He came close and said to Mark to follow him. They stopped few meters away.

While they were talking I filled my belt with 40 bullets that I wasted on the air and for the target shooting.

## CHAPTER EIGHTEEN

We moved again with out learning about the distance of Albertville.

After about 30 minutes, Jean's Jeep stopped again. He waived us to carry on, as they had to go back for refueling...

To my question of why they went back, Mark said without looking at me, that they would re-join us later.

As I was the only one of our companions who spoke English and could communicate with Mark; many times I had to keep quiet of not to worry them about my doubtfulness concerning Jean and Mark...

This time, again I kept it to myself, as I was almost certain, but I had no evidence, that Jean was going to execute the colorful officer...

With Mark on the steering we carried on. He had to be extra careful, because the road was getting worse and worse, with loose rocks shooting left - right. Some times the road was very narrow...

Suddenly at a sharp turn, an opening appears, with a truck that was abandon at the side of the road.

We stopped and Mark went to investigate.

With his gun in his hand, he walked slowly around it.

I was out of the Jeep with my mashing gun ready when he called me to go there.

I told the men to come out and get cover behind the Jeep, with their guns ready.

I walked towards the truck. It looked fairly new. It was a Ford (Petrol) 3 – ton. It could be more or less 2 to 3 years old. Before I come closed, I noticed through the open rear door, of some metal things shinning. I climbed up from the rear steel door to see what was in side and... I had another shock. This time could be very serious. I call

Mark to come up from the side. He managed to climb up and after about of three shocking minutes, he jumped down and went on the side of the road and started vomiting…

Of what I saw in front of me, scattered around, were about: One dozen long dirty knives, full of blood. About twelve swords, like those using to cut - open bushes and branches for opening paths inside the Jungle; they were also covered with blood - stains. Closed to a thousand bullets…where half of them were used…

Also, five Knob - Kerrie's (Knob - Kerrie was a stick about one meter long, where at the end of it had a knob like a Knuckle Duster, with a knife pierced through it. All the knives were covered with poisonous).

Also five Pipes, for shooting poisonous darts, by blowing.

More than I could count were Bows with poisonous Arrows.

All of those and many other metal and wooded staff, all covered by some blood.

I couldn't count of course how many hundreds of flies were there.

Thank God, there were no dead bodies on the truck!

I jumped down fill really sick and opened the driver's door… There again, blood was all over the seat, with somebody tried to clean it up, or pulled out a dead body.

Mark shouted at me to be careful of what I touched, as it could be poison spread on it.

Holding my breath I tried to function properly my nerve system. That happened when I looked under the bloody dashboard to see if everything was in its place.

Not surprisingly I saw all the wires connecting to the ignition switch had been cut, with somebody tried to re connected them again, but the only success they did was to burn out some fuses.

I opened the cambium (the small cabinet) and I find a pair of pliers, a screwdriver and some mechanical tools, where in the hands of an experience mechanic, could be very useful.

I got out and opened the bonnet, to look if the battery was in order. I opened the battery cups hopping to find some liquid in it. I noticed that it only needed was some steel water.

I clime up and in front of all the men I urine in side the little holes, but I needed more...I call them all to do the same, if they want me to start the truck.

Mark went up first and the rest of the men after him. We all laughed as they tried hard to find the hole...

This laughter made all of as to ease the tension we had so many hours of no sleep and no food. I advise the men not to go and see of what was on top of the truck, but slowly – slowly, all the men went up and see for themselves.

The men, during the time I was working with Gino as my assistant, they were trying to communicate between themselves by telling Sophocles experience with the black Girl back in Kamina and his desire to have her all - night...

After I replaced the cups, I went to the back of the truck and I cut off with the pliers a piece of wire, which was going to the rear lights. I connected it to the one side to the positive pole of the battery and the other side to the coil. In that manner, I had current to the points.

I opened them (the points) with the screwdriver and to my pleasant surprise I saw that spark was coming. It wasn't very strong, but it was there!

I disconnected the wire from the battery, so I don't have to waist the little electricity, and by using the screwdriver first, and the pliers after as a tool, I took off the air cleaner.

To make it short, I cleaned the carburetor as much as I could and after I saw that the fuel was going through, then, I placed back the filter on it.

I came down and went back to the fuel tank to see how much petrol (Gas) was in it. The tap opened easy. I went to the bushes and pull some branches out. I clean one that looked long enough to make it a stick. I submerged the stick in to the tank. After I checked it, I said to Mark who was next to me, that we had petrol for about 200 kilometers.

When I took the tap to place it back to the tank, I noticed some sand on it.

"Mark, wait a minute! There is a possibility that some body threw sand in to the tank. You know what can happen if it had to go to the cylinders?"

"Yes I do!" Mark said quickly. "What we do now?"

"You can pull me with a Jeep and I hope I will started, then, we will turn it slowly to deliver it to the Soldiers back at the camp and I will explain to them of what to do."

Although he gave orders to two South Africans to pull me with a rope, he appeared to be unwilling to help.

At that time when the men were getting the rope to tight to the two bumpers of the Jeep and the Truck, then, Jean appears with his Jeep, followed by another Jeep.

With out saying anything, the men from the other Jeep dropped three of 20litter canisters of fuel (but no food) and they returned back. Jean stopped further down and called Mark. He runs to him and after a short chat Mark came back telling us to go and scan the area. Something that we should have done it few times...

I took another belt full of bullets and put it around my shoulder.

We split in two groups again, on both the sides of the road, with our guns ready.

In that manner and without a word to each other, we scanned the area for about fifteen minutes. Then, the `Captains' told us, to return.

I hold my nerves back and smiled instead, when I asked him if somebody was guarding the Jeep, where if by any chance the Rebels were hiding in the Jungle and waiting for us to leave, then we could loose the Jeep and would have been alone in the Jungle, praying for Jean and his company to come to meet us, before we die from Jungle diseases or from hunger…

"Mark! I said to him. Look here!"

He looked, to see me holding the keys of the Jeep.

"Oh, George, thanks God, I clean forgot about the keys…"

He run and embraced me.

Before he went back to his position I whispered in his ear.

"Not so lucky though! Because if they couldn't steel it, they can burn it or damage it!"

Mark thanked me once again and shouted to one of the skinny South Africans:

"Hey John, run as fast as you can to the Jeep and guard it with your life"

After gave his `order' then, Mark turned to the others and said:

"Follow me men! Follow me!"

When we came back, Mark willingly this time, went to the Jeep ready to pull me at my command…

I connected the wire to the battery and signal him to go, while I had the second gear engaged and the clutch pressed down.

After few minutes I let go the clutch and press slightly the accelerator pedal. It started immediately.

I took the gear out and with my left foot I pressed the brakes to stop it, while with my right foot rave the engine (not so much), so, to warm it up.

I signal to Mark using my thump up, to loose the rope.

Before I reversed the truck back into the open, I saw 2 Jeep coming with Jean in one of them. Both the Jeep was full of men, stopping there, celebrating with the others. When I approached them I could hear them happily laughing and shouting, with every one uses his own language.

While Mark was pulling the truck, I noticed that on the clock, there were only 10 000 kilometers, which means that the truck could be one year old.

While we all celebrated our first success in Africa and before I come out of the truck, all of a sudden from no were, armed men in camouflage uniform appeared, from all angles.

I do not know what happened to me, as I felt guilty and inexperience, because my gun was not at my side, but resting on top of the front seat of the Jeep.

Without thinking, I looked in front of me to find the most gathered `enemies` and I attack them, by putting the first gear and accelerated like I was going to the a races, spinning the rear wheels.

Thanks God, I heard Mark shouting at the `enemy` in English, to move to the side of the road (Left).

Of course nobody moved, as they didn't understand him, and also they did not have the time, because moving to the side was a muddy up hill as well.

But, if they couldn't do anything, I could!

Marks words alerted me, as there was no `enemy`. As I hit the brakes, at the same time I swing the steering to the opposite side of the group.

Lucky for all of us, I didn't harm anyone.

With the engine running, I got out of the truck and grub George from his sleeve, asking him to explain to the shocking men, that I didn't know they were regular Soldiers.

Thanks to my reflexes, I am still alive, as if I had hit or kill one man, then, dozens of machine guns, would be aimed and shoot with out stopping, finishing their magazines on me!

I don't know about the others, but Jean, who had changed to another uniform, with a blue silk scarf around his neck, wouldn't do anything to save my skin. As for Mark, who shouted at the black Soldiers, he did that, not to save their lives, but his own skin; as if they had shot me, then both would prefer to surrender, instead of risking their miserable skins to lift their guns to avenge me…

The Soldiers and the man in command, who was another colorful Captain, looked like they understood, as they were more interested about the truck, than me.

By the way! Of what happened to the first colorful Captain I cannot write about it, because since the first time, I never saw him again.

Through George, I talked to two men, suppose to be technicians, that the battery needed proper charging, saw them and explain to them of what to do with the wires, and how to take the tank and all the piping out and clean them up…

Of what I could gather, they understood me; who was going to do the work, was one thing, and how they could find parts for the ignition switch, was another.

With me driving the truck, we all return back to the camp.

Although was eleven thirty in the morning; the temperature was closed to 40 degrees Celsius, with all of us men from Marks Jeep, had never slept and eat for over 15 hours of driving through the Jungle and through night…

Another irrational incident that was funny but not so funny happened to us, in the middle of the unfriendly Congo.

About an hour after we arrived at the camp, I noticed a two - engine Dakota circling around us, to drop some FOOD. According to Mark there should be some small and big tin containers of food.

To our surprise the side door of the Dakota opened suddenly and three men pushed two wooden boxes with out a parachute, with the result the boxes broke up with a hell of a bang, scattering our precious food all over the Jungle, with most of the cans to be broken and opened…

Into our effort of us men (20 all and all) to find our food, we had another 25 to 30 of the 200 Soldiers and 4 Captains looking inside the thick and thorny bushes; although they had an Antelope hanging upside down on four large logs, with fire burning underneath it. Apart of the Antelope, they had on top of another fire, a large pot with beans in it, boiling.

Looking at the huge pot, one could think if they used it for something else; like a white meat for example. Just to think of that, nobody went to taste the beans or the Antelope.

I was ready to give up when I find `hidden and…intact in the bushes` a 5 - liter can.

With out seen what was written on it, I opened it with my bayonet and…of what I saw in it, I would never forget it as long as I leave…

Can you imagine, in the middle of a dessert, when you are ready to drop from thirst, to find a 5 - liter cool mixed fruit, with a lot of juice, telling you with the sweetest kind words; "Please eat me up! Please swallow me down!"

Well, I always had good manners, and so, I lifted the can and let the sweet and tasty cool juice coming down to my throat, along with most of the mixed fruit. While I was swallowing them down, I hard myself roaring like a Lion attacking its prairie, and if I had to compare it with the pleaser of sex, then, sex was coming second best (at least at this very moment…)…

After few minutes, when I realized that I consumed all the juice and half of the mixed fruit, only then I looked at my stomach and my belly. Of what I saw, had nothing to do with my well maintain 65 kilogram, muscular body. I saw an ugly balloon, ready to blow at the touch of a needle.

Of what was left out of the most wonderful magic box in the Jungle of Congo, I took it in my arms with the greatest of care, promising to guide it with my life. Then I closed the top and I went about twenty meters deep in the Jungle, where was a little river. I place it in between two little rocks, closed to the water, then I cut some wide leafs and I cover it, thus, it would be far way from evil eye, even from the sun.

I gave it a name. I called it, Theo - Thora. Theo, means `God`, when Thora means `Gifts`, so, `God's Gifts.
`

Quietly I moved towards the camp, promising to my Theodora that I will visit it and very soon.

On my way I met with Sof, where he had consumed the food of broken cans, along with dirt, because his mouth around his lips was green and brown.

He was sweating and looked like he had fever. He wanted water!

Unwillingly I took him to the river while I asked him if he had his pill for yellow fever with him. He said he did!

Without hesitation he jumped in, but quickly came out, asking me if I saw any Crocodile...

I fill up with water his canteen and mine.

Before we return to the camp, I waved goodbye to my Theodora, as by the looks of it I will not see her again!

When we arrived, I noticed with a great surprise that they had not only already cleaned the truck, but they had and placed on top of the carriage, two large steel benches for the Soldiers to seat on. I couldn't believe it; they did it so fast, like they had the benches hidden behind the trees...

The engine was still running.

In order to explain to the black Soldier who by the looks of it was the driver, I looked for Jean but he was sleeping on top of some fresh cut tree leaves, so, I called George the Belgium.

I explained and showed him to tell the driver about how to disconnect and connect again the wire from the battery to the coil and by using the screwdriver, of how to start the engine. Explain again about cleaning the tank as soon as possible and all the fuel pipes and fuel filter as well.

I took him inside the truck and saw him the wires and what wires needed temporarily, until they replace the complete ignition switch? Also if could get a new battery.Then, I switched the engine off.

After that, I tried to get some sleep also on top of some tree - leaves, but was impossible. I rested my tired body any way.

## CHAPTER NINETEEN

At four o'clock, we told to move again.

We started, by me driving Jeans Jeep with him next to me. From this side I could see his swollen cheek and his left damaged arm heavily bandaged.

After few minutes of driving, I noticed that Jean was...crying.

I stopped the Jeep, as I couldn't bear to see this man of so much hate for revenge, to cry from frustration.

I beg him to listen without interrupting me:

"I understand your hate for the blacks and if I were in your place, most probably I would feel the same, but to hate those blacks where you voluntarily signed up to help, even risking your life, it doesn't make any sense..."

It looked like I convinced Jean, because he listened carefully while he was looking at me.

He wiped off his tears with the back of his right hand and said:

"George, you are right, but I cannot help it not to hate these bastards..."

He wanted to say something else, but he turned his face to the other side and kept quite...

Definitely this man is holding back something that is more horrible than the killing of his parents!

We find the truck not so far away from the camp, with the Soldiers and some of our men around it, with their guns ready to shoot (the Soldiers). As soon as they saw me going to the truck, they started talking between themselves, keep pointing their guns towards me.

As I had no gun, I pretended that I didn't see anything...

With a quick look on the points, I noticed that there wasn't any major problem, as the engine was cut off and they couldn't start it again.

As no one could tell me of what happened I took the opportunity with the few tools that I had to clean the carburetor and the air cleaner from the mad again.

As long as I was working, I took off again the wire from the coil to the battery, because it could be dangerous of burning the condenser and the coil as well.

I went to the bushes and I cut a long branch from something that appears to be like a sugar cane...I cleaned it with my bayonet and went to the tank to check the fuel again.

"It has fuel for about 100 kilometers," I said to Jean.

I connected again the wire and started the engine with the screwdriver. I worm it up and went inside taking the steering.

I `order` Jean to bring me my gear and my gun, because I couldn't leave the accelerator.

When he brought them, I said to him:

"I! Will drive this truck! Please tell them!"

The Soldiers, before even Jean finished his translation to them, they started jumping on the truck shouting with joy, with some of them pointing the thump up. They were about twenty-five men.

Jean called George to seat next to me, as he would drive the Jeep.

The time was six - thirty p.m. and the night was coming rapidly.

More than an hour of drive with first and second gear, we reached an opening where I noticed an abandon smaller truck. I stopped with out cutting the engine and I went to investigate, in case I could find some fuel in it. I delayed about fifteen minutes to transfer few liters of petrol /gas, because nobody was helping me and I had no proper containers and piping…

So, the ride to hell was continued, with the road to be worse than before.

I had to use the lights, where thank God, they were working.

Apart of the non - existed road, an unusual phenomenon appeared all of a sudden in front of our eyes, where either the City or Country boys weren't really ready for this shocking experience…

In front of us, about 30 to 40 meters, I noticed a black flat thing, lying down on the gravel road. Before I applied the brakes, the black thing moved towards us, not walking… but…flying. I shouted to the Soldiers to be careful, but nobody heard me. It came direct to strike the windscreen of the truck, but it lifted itself and it strikes the glass, not with its body, but with its 3 meters long funny tale. Lucky the windscreen came out intact.

After that shock, then, I heard the Soldiers, where some of them were laughing and some were screaming.

The `Phenomenon`, made a circle around us and as it passed us from the right side, while its tail was hitting the top of the trees and brunches, I had a good look at it. It looked like a black Flying Saucer… with a tail.

After few minutes of drive, I heard the black Soldiers to complain of something and they started bagging the top of the truck to stop. Before I stop I looked through the rear view mirror to see how closed the two Jeep were behind us.

At this very moment, the engine looked like it was going to stop, telling me in the mechanical language that this was the end of the road, as the petrol was almost finished.

Before the engine cuts off, I put it to neutral and I applied the brakes with my left foot, because with my right I rev the engine on and off, as if it had to turn off, then, it would be impossible to stop the truck, as the air-hydraulic brake system wouldn't work. Eventually came to halt. I pulled the handbrake.

Before I even opened the door to get out, the black Soldiers had already vanished in the awful quiet Jungle. Naturally, nobody carried any flashlight at all…

I went around to the tank and after few kicks it told me to pass my time with something more useful, instead of kicking it, as it was empty!

Now, where the black Soldiers weren't there to saw us the way to Albertville, I left it to the great leaders Mark and Jean, but I took charge of our transportation.

We were 12 men, split them in half of 6 men to every Jeep.

From the spare container, I took petrol to the first Jeep that I was going to drive it.

I complain to Mark to let somebody to help me with the other Jeep.

Eventually Jack filled up the other, telling me:

"Sorry George"

Before we moved, I took `liberty` to ask Jean of how far we were from Albertville.

He looked at me and he said:

"George, I really do not know yet…" and he walked away towards Mark.

After one hour of drive, with the full moon shinning up on the sky, our two Jeep convoy of following one another, with only food and water dropped from the sky…, at last we stopped to rest and to sleep.

The time was 9.30 p.m.

We placed guards every hour. I fall a sleep as soon as I closed my eyes.

They woke me up at midnight.

To past the shivering night in the Hell of Congo with my gun in my hands, I started of doing some exercises, using my bayonet as an attack and my body and my gun as a defense. Those movements came so naturally to me like somebody was directing my entire body and mind, to protect me from a dangerous attack and to retaliate in a manner that will not kill…

"Am I made for this kind of fighting?" I said to myself, in the middle of the night and in the middle of Africa.

`In case in the end I will pull through from this adventure, then, I will use this kind of talent, to fight crime and terror, where ever it will comes from`

I woke up the next guard, which was Sof.

Soon I felt the cold and I went to the Jeep where I had my gear and took a woolen sweater. I set on the co-drivers seat, covering my body with our personal blanket.

Before I closed my eyes, I looked around and through the clean sky with full moon I noticed that around the Jeep on the ground, all the men were covering themselves with their personal blanket.

Two of my Italian friends had slept back to back, thus, they were using two blankets to cover them up.

Soon I fall a sleep, with my gun in my hands… but at 2 - 45 a.m. (I saw the time at the phosphorous watch, we all had), some noise woke me up. I kept my breath and with out moving my head I looked around to pin - point the noise.

Not surprisingly, I saw Mark next to the Jeep, shivering, to that extent that his teeth were rattling. For a moment I thought that he had a stroke, but in actual fact, he was filling cold.

He placed his hands in side where the men had their gear, looking for something.

I thought he was looking for an extra blanket.

He moved his hands towards me.

While he felt and grabbed my blanket, his teeth were rattling again, but my hands were resisting, of depriving their precious material.

I said to him quietly:

"Mark, there is a human under this fuc... blanket!"

Like he was hit by a lightning, he jumped back, saying: "Sorry"

He searched behind the seat as he was looking for something specific. In the end he found a small metal bottle of brandy where he had hidden it all the time... I did not say anything this time.

I fall a sleep again practicing in my dream with God Aries those techniques I did when I was guarding, having Goddess Athena as our only spectator; then... I heard a massing - gun, almost next to my ears. The noise was so loud in the quiet night, it sounded into my ears like I was inside a bell...

I jumped out of the Jeep with my gun ready. I looked around to find the enemy, but thank God wasn't any enemy, but... Mark!

The idiot of a man, because he couldn't get warm by his brandy, he felt better to awake all of us in this way. If by any change there were Baloumba (Rebels) at more than one kilometer away, then, they will be waiting for us further down to eat us for breakfast...

Further more, he was wasting ammunition again.

Instead of swearing at him in English and Greek, I started getting ready. The same did all the other men, but every one was not only swearing at him but swearing at themselves as well, for accepting this adventure in the Hell of the Congo…

As for the word: In the Hell of the Congo, I supported them all the way!

With out thinking, I said to Mark:

"Mark, now that you woke us up, even by this unusual manner, before we move on, can I do the men some warm up exercises, because of the weather…"

"Yes! Yes!" Mark said, and started jumping up and down…

I did warm up exercises for about 15 minutes. All the techniques, all the movements and all the combinations, I never had done them before, even at the time of practicing with some Japanese Masters where occasionally were coming to the UK to teach the Instructors and give black belt grading. It was like I had an invisible Instructor moving my hands and feet.

Eventually at 4 o clock in the morning, we started again for our Journey to Albertville.

After about one hour, we entered a little Town with beautiful cottage houses, some shops and a church as well. We stop out of the church and instead of a priest, we saw a white American War Journalist from the a Movie company for News coming out, holding a professional movie camera, with two large black bags hanging around his neck.

This man where his name was Jim, came all the way to the Congo voluntarily to take pictures and movies for the world to learn of what was going on in these parts of Africa.

We took him with us. When Mark offered him one of his two revolvers he carried with him, he refused.

On our way out of the village, I noticed abandoned many cars of different make, left on the streets. All of them had something damaged, like a front suspension, damaged radiator, puncture tires, broken windscreens, etc. I thought that the Rebels, where the Soldiers used to call them `Balumba` (as I mentioned above), did all these damages to the fairly new model motorcars.

I hard some people shooting and shouting from the back Jeep, but it was falls alarm, with Jean been the star, shooting at a monkey, thought was a Balumba.

We took Jim in Jeans car and we moved on...

After some time, I noticed Mark who was seating next to me, looking very worried, even ignored the loud conversation between the Italians in the back of the Jeep.

The road was getting slightly better, but still awful narrow and shooting loosing rocks left - right...

The time was seven fifteen, with the sun already out and in front of my eyes.

Suddenly and without any warning of our two super Heroes, we entered a clean down hill tar road.

Before I realized the changing of the road, I had to turn to the right... and then... in front of my eyes... a modern and up to date Fairly big City, with a large sunken square, appeared, with Lake Albertville seen as a back ground, at about 4 - 5 kilometers away.

In and around of the square were planted many and deferent kind of trees.

In the middle of the park - like square, was the 5 - story hotel, where we were after, to save the hostages, as we told at Kamina base.

Connecting the hotel from the road where we were standing right now, was a magnificent piece of architecture in a shape of a staircase, made from granite, measuring about 5 meters long, going in to the square and about 5 meters wide, on top of the road.

From the left and from right side of the staircase, in front of us, were three poles on one side and three one the other side, carved on a white stone, with each one been about one meter height above the ground and about two meters apart of each other.

I run and took cover behind of one of those poles that was next to the left of the staircase, so did the other men of my Jeep. As for the Jeep it self, was `parked` in the middle of the road.

First I heard, then, I saw about 45 to 50 Balumba shouting and screaming in front of the door of the hotel. Most of them were carrying Bows and Arrows and the rest carrying those Flat Swords and Blow Darts...

I noticed that they were waiving their weapons, like they wanted to tell us something.

I look for Jean and his men, but I couldn't see them. His Jeep was empty behind ours.

Mark who was next to me said that Jean took his men from the other side that could have a good look at the road that was leading to the Lake...

He also told me to tell the Greeks to aim and fire at will, but they must aim at the head.

He said the same to Gino who was on the other side...

From my position, although the sun was in my eyes, I could see that nobody had shot at us any arrows or anything else, so, I didn't shoot them, but I... saw them dropping on the ground, one by one, from the bullets of my comrades.

Out of all the shooting, I counted 4 dead and 2 were down to their knees, but nobody went to hide and nobody started shooting any Arrows at us.

I shouted at Mark:

"Maybe they want to surrender."

His white - white skin turned to red cheek, with his nose more red at the end, revealing the nose of an alcoholic...

As Jean was nowhere around, and under my pressure, he told the men to stop shooting.

I looked at George and I waived at him to follow us, to communicate with the Balumba. While George hesitates, Mark starts getting down the stares with me to be two steps behind him...

Suddenly, hell broke, as somebody from the one window of the hotel, started shooting at us with a mashing - gun. Lucky for both of us, the bullets didn't touch us at all, but damaged some steps in front of our legs...

I reacted like a lightning...

I took one step upwards and flew over the stairs, somersaulting on the air, with out leaving my mashing - gun. I hit the road with my boots and dive behind the same pole I was earlier, dropping the uncomfortable helmet, which it stopped few meters away.

Mark swearing at me about four different kinds of swearing words while he sawed me his shirt that had a hole on the left sleeve, but the bullet didn't touch his flesh.

He took cover behind the same pole he was before, ordering us to:

"Shoot and kill all the black caffirs!" (I think `caffir` is a swearing word to the South African blacks).

Maybe Mark escaped injury, but George who was opposite than me on the other side of the stairs, `received` a bullet on top of his shoulder:

"Giorgo" He shouted at me. "I have been wounded on my shoulder!" (Giorgo is my Greek name).

Inside his bad luck, the injury wasn't that serious, as the bullet only damaged the top of his left shoulder, not touching a bone, or a tendon, but burned it, like someone touched it with a hot iron - bar...

I apologized to Mark, but I didn't shoot the Balumba who were at the door - step of the hotel, becoming less and less in numbers, but I aimed at the window…

Before I started shooting, I looked to see which one could be the one who shot us. I noticed some smoke from one window, then, I heard 3 shots. Two of them strike the stairs, but one hit the side of the Jeep, very closed to the spare fuel container (I saw it later on).

With out taking my eyes out of that window, I aim and let go also three bullets towards the smock of that window.

"No more bullets out of that nasty window against us," I said to George, smiling, trying to relieve him from his pain…

I don't know if I killed them, or kill the one who shot us, but since then, it appeared that I won the fight between my conscious and the raw reality of staying alive in the Hell of the Congo's Jungle at any cost, which means; better alive than dead, as I was to young to die!

There at the Hotel, were about ten opened windows, facing us, so, every time before I went to the next one, I made sure that I closed for good the previous one.

While I was doing my stupid duty as a Soldier of Piece, I made a pledge to myself, that if I will come out intact, I will try to prevent any young foolish for entering any kind of war-like adventure…Trying to teach him the values of life and the respect of the individual as such.

## CHAPTER TWENTY

Now dear Reader, we are moving in our time, as at the end of the first part, we left a united family, where they are still sitting in the same library, with Master G.K. talking:

"Looking through the Diary, my memories are coming back very fast and alive, like it happened yesterday, although, thirty - three"…
"Thirty - three years had past!" said simultaneously, Artemis, G.K. and Persa, like they were one person.

They all laughed…

G.K. and Persa, sitting on lotus position next to each other on the thick Oriental carpet, facing their parents, where Artemis, was still sitting on the arm chair next to her life long love and Father of her Son. She so afraid to loose him, that she still holding his palm with her two hands, making very difficult for him to turn the pages of the black Diary. She still looking at him in his eyes; even trying not to blink…
"Shihan, I mean Father; what happened at the hotel after the mashing gun from the windows stopped?"
"Son, don't stop calling me Father, even in the competition area. My South African friends and our rivals will love it, because you are not only a student any more, but my flesh and blood, so the pain of loosing all their fights to you will give less pain… But when we are together like now, you can call me… Dad, and this is not a command but I need it so much to hear it from my Sons mouth…"

"I remember Dad" says G.K. (knowing his long time pain of not having a child of his own). "I remember when you were giving black belt grading to those they had to go a way for their army duty or to move to another city, how said you were, like you were loosing your own children…"

"So you noticed that as well?" The Father said to his Son.

He then turned to Artemis, asking her:

"Artemis, did you fill the same as me, although you have Persa calling you Mom?"

She is not in a position to answer, but… she releases his hand and throws herself on to him, embracing him around his neck with both her arms, whispering in his ear, loud enough, so her Son could listen to her:

"As I told you earlier, I saw our Son when he was 10 years old in the orphanage, when Mrs. Maria so wisely at that time, told me not to talk to him, but, I could give my life to hear our son calling me Mom."

After those words, she gives him a quick kiss in his mouth and contracts her hands from his neck and grabs his left palm again with both her hands, squeezing it…

"Artemis! Only death will separate us now!" The Master just said, not only feeling the grip over his palm, but also felt the agony from her rising pulses.

With his free right hand, opens the Diary, which it was resting on his lap. He looks quickly through it…

He is focusing his eyes in front of nowhere and talking to himself, said:

"Since then my life changed completely"

Then he started reading from his dairy again:

From that window, I never saw any movement again. So, I looked, focused and shoot at any `window` that tried to kill us, until all the windows were `shut. `

Some how satisfied that I won this battle against the hidden Rebels, my consciousness started bothering me again …, as I turned my eyes to those Balumba left in front of the door of the hotel, but… they were vanished, taking with them all the dead and wounded. I couldn't believe it in my eyes.

I quick changed magazine (the fourth one), then, holding the mashing - gun in my arms, I dive at my left on the tar – road and grab my helmet with my left hand.

At this particular second, living my post where supposed I `shut` all the windows down, that second, saved my life, as a barrage of bullets struck the top of the pole-post where I was behind it a second earlier, shuttering it into pieces, leaving only half of it. Parts of the pieces hit my back, but not a scratch…

I turned my body so, that I was facing the sky with my gun and my helmet in my hands, thanking God, in the face of Christ. I could not help it but into in to my mind also came the face of Goddess Athena, but I imagined her as an Angel, sent to save me by God!

"Did you free the hostages? Artemis asks him.

"No! Not only we did not freed them, but also we never saw or learned about their whereabouts, or if they were ever existed! Only we had some roomers, or possibly they had removed them from the hotel…"

Master G.K. commands the Robot in English to come close and he takes a glass of orange juice, offering it to Artemis, telling her:

"I remember!"

"And so do I" Artemis said and she gets up, offering him lemonade.

G.K. knowing how Shihan's hospitality works, he gets up asking Persa, what she wants to drink.

Persa, without saying anything, points out at the lemonade. G.K. takes the two last glasses, offering first to Persa, keeping the last orange for himself.

Without any warning, the Robot starts moving away to the kitchen…

"What we will have for dinner?" G.K. asks in Greek, knowing the answer.

Without stopping, the Robot answers also in Greek: "Surprise, Surprise!"

G.K. waits until the robot is at a reasonable distance and tells Persa:

"Normally it doesn't talk or answer's to anybody else, except my Father. I thought it was going to swear at me, but this time it was kind to me, possibly because we have visitors…

My Father brought me one Robot to my home in Dionysus (area like Malibu in the USA). This particular Robot listens to me, but when I am not precise, it will swear at me in 5 different languages.

"What do you mean, about precise?" Persa asks smiling.

"Not to interrupt my Father. I will tell you quickly an example: In case I have programmed it to make dinner at 8 o clock in the evening and I will come home ten minutes later, then it will tell me:"

"If you want hot dinner, then you must go and have a cold shower."

"Above that, I must do 100 push – ups, and in case I do not wash my hands again, then, in the kitchen, the steel chair with the leather cover that I will seat, will be frozen in winter and very- very hot in the summer, as it happened few times to me in South Africa ... I will tell you more later..."

G.K. apologizes to his Father, expecting to find his stern - look, but he sees him smiling and understanding, waiting patently for his Son to finish...

G.K. bows to him, taking a deep breather, thinking that from now on, he will always have that kind of affection, where he and his Father missed so much...

After almost they all finished their juices; the three asked the Master to continue.

"We were left at the time where the pole - post was shattered." Persa said!

Reading from the Diary

`After my quick thanks to God, I looked at the windows again. I noticed that the very first window had some smock inside, but as usual, I never saw anybody, as it was dark. I aim at few spots inside of it and I let go about 20 bullets. I thought 20 bullets were my retaliation for striking the pole - post. I call it pole-post, as I do not know any other name of it...

Dead silence again!

George, since the time he was wounded, he couldn't shoot, but he was looking at me all the time, possibly to attend his wound:

"You cleaned up the real Balumba, while we killed the poor Rebels, who had no guns to shoot us." He said that, and turned his face to Mark who told us to shoot all the blacks, swearing at him, in Greek and France.

Before Mark was loosing his color again, Jean with the others came running to us...

"Come George let's go, let's go! Thousands of Balumba are coming from the lake. They will be here in ten - fifteen minutes!"

I explained quickly in Greek and Gino in Italian…

It was going to be a panic; I save it again by entering into the Jeep, tell Mark and the others to come in, but I couldn't see Sof. When I call his name I saw him getting up from inside of the other Jeep, where by the looks of it, he never used his gun at all. Instead of coming to my Jeep, he stayed there, holding his gun in front of his chest.

Jean anticipate me, by telling and doing the same thing with his men…

I tried to take 360-degree turn and followed the same road I was coming, because there were three roads exactly the same.

As I was going to accelerate, Mark who was sitting next to me, shouted to look at my left side. At the same time he was trying to aim and shoot, through my face. When he swing his hands from the right to the left, the bat of the gun strike the dashboard and a bullet came pass my face…

"Sorry George," he said again.

I didn't say anything because nothing happened to me, but I strike his gun out of my face and I pulled the handbrake.

I looked and I saw two - dragged Balumba coming (Jogging) towards us.

The one on the left was holding a Bow and Arrow, ready to let it go… As for the other, he was holding one of those poisoned flat swords.

While jogging, they both were shouting those words:

"My mullele, my mullele;" means: The Bullet is Water.

These two `dangerous` Balumba, who were coming to us without been in a hurry, Mark gets up and from inside the Jeep, aims and shout, all the bullets he had in his magazine, without touching no one. He looses his color again.

I told him to seat down as I aim on the head of one of them, because while running he was going to let the poisonous arrow go, aiming at us.

He stopped like he was hitting by a truck. The distance was about 50 miters away.

The other Balumba was so drugged that he didn't even looked at his side. He carried on coming to us, shouting the same words…

Somebody from the back of the Jeep (it was Gino) let go a barrage of bullets at him. Most of them got him at both his legs, but one of them killed him. I looked at the back and saw Gino wiping his tears off, made me think that I wasn't the only one who hated this bloody war.

I looked at the hotel and didn't see any move, so, I got out of the Jeep and walk towards the two dead Balumba, ignoring Marks ordering me to come back.

I ignored him because I noticed something was hanging from the neck of both the dead Balumba.

I took a deep breath of relief as I saw that they both had explosives around their half naked body, but not one bullet had strike them.

Before I say fair - well to the `African Kamikaze`, I took carefully the Bow and one Arrow… I could see clearly the poison at the edge – point of it.

I run back because they all were shouting at me to go.

Another comical-tragic incident happened in the middle of the Jungle

Lucky for Jean and his men I delayed our departure, because he saw us leaving, as they were returning from taking a wrong road.

Just as well for them, as they were leading themselves into a dead - end.

When Jean realized that he took wrong direction, told Jack to return immediately. As Jack tried to do a fast U turn on a very narrow road with a 200 meters cliff at his left and right side, he didn't realized that Sof was falling out of the Jeep, nearly going over the cliff, to be breakfast for the ever hungry for white meat Balumba.

Sof was running behind the Jeep screaming to stop.

With the help of the men, they pulled him inside while Jean and Jack felt didn't care a less if he was left behind…

When I saw the Jeep, I waived at them, signaling to follow me.

As soon as they were closed to us and I started moving up hill, I noticed Sof jumping out of the Jeep, willingly this time, shouting at me in Greek to stop…

"Giorgo, my friend, stop the fu… Jeep"

When I stop and he jumped in, he came and seat direct behind me, pushing Gino away.

I pressed the accelerator and changed to second gear, when I saw and felt Sof's right arm around my neck, squeezing my throat, while his other arm was holding the parallel bar, thus making it more difficult for me to breath.

Of course I couldn't drive, but I tried to hold as much as possible, thinking of Sof not to have a heart attack, because he had high palpitation, and his body smell like burning fat, where even the Balumba couldn't eat it…

I was going to strike (gently) his right eye with my left index finger, when Mark beat me to the second.

He took out his revolver and placed it to Sof's throat, under his jaw, pressing the carotid artery very hard, forcing Sof to release the grip.

Mark, while pressed his gun, shouted at Sof in English:

"Let go, or you are fuc... dead!"

The presser of the revolver made Sof to scream from pain, but never the less, he retracted his damn arm from my throat.

I cough a little, but I was O.K.

We must of have been driving for about five to eight minutes, leaving the road and entering again the gravel - narrow torture.

While I was looking through the rear view mirror (at the side of the door) to look if the Jeep was following us, I didn't realize what happened in the front, but as soon as I was going to turn my head on to the road, I noticed that Mark wasn't next to me...

I looked back and none of the men were there as well...

I looked at the road in front of me and...I swing the steering to the left and hit the brakes. I pulled the handbrake very hard, almost breaking the cable. My heart started doing somersaults in my chest when I jumped out of the Jeep, from the co-drivers side, with the mashing - gun in my hands...

There, in the middle of the road, about 100 Balumba were blocking our escape, shouting `my moullele`and jogging towards me, with their usual weaponry in their hands.

I let three bullets at them, while I heard dozens of bullets were coming from the back of the other Jeep.

I looked behind my Jeep and I see no one. This is to have comrades to support you in the middle of the Jungle, with your life at stake.

Holding my gun with both hands I dive backwards, doing a Judo roll, loosing again the damn helmet. By rolling my body on the road I managed to get cover behind the Jeep, not alone, as I hade 4 magazines of 20 bullets each and two belts around me as well. Certainly I would reserve one bullet for my dry head, instead of getting captured and be eaten by those maniacs, where thanks God they were coming at me very slowly, but surely, closing the distance.

I placed my left knee on the ground and I started shooting, but I didn't see anybody falling.

Without leaving them out of my eyesight, I finished the first and the second magazine shooting one by one, aiming for the head.

I quickly changed to a third one from my shirts pocket. Of what I could see from behind the Jeep, the Balumba were still coming and they must of have been close to ten meters away:

"This is the end," I said loudly in Greek to myself.

I aim and before I started shooting again, I heard one, then another... defensive grenades, which they were thrown, by the two Italians (One was my friend Gino) where they were behind some Huts, next to the second Jeep. Lucky they dropped them in the middle of the bundle.

Strait after that I heard another grenade explosion, but the bang was from behind of the Jeep...

The two grenades not only made a tremendous bang, but made an effective impact on the `enemy` as well.

Thank God, after this bang with a lot of fire and smock, made the Balumba running into the Jungle from all directions, leaving this time the dead and the wounded behind them.

With the finger ready to pull the trigger, I tried to look through the smock, but I couldn't see anything. I was eager to look behind to the other Jeep, but something or somebody was telling me not to do it… and I kept looking in front.

"That something was Goddess Athena, Father?" asks G.K so natural again of not calling him with his Japanese title's name, as he had done it for so many years in the past.

"Yes my Son!" The Master also replied. Getting used to it, like his Son…

"Thanks to Goddess Athena I am alive and well and find my family, although for so many years I suffered so much; but the little time that I am with you and your Mother, it replaces all the suffering of loneliness and unhappiness I went through in South Africa. Although the last 11 years when I had you with me, it was like I had you adopted, as I was teaching you everything I was creating. You know that, many times, when I was showing you a fighting technique for competition, and I was watching you to use it so effectively, I felt like I was myself fighting…"

"And every time I scored on my opponent, using your unique scoring technique, you were turning your back and went to find any object to go behind it, to hind your emotions and your tears; coming back quickly to do the same, after I scored again!"

"So you new it, how did you notice it? You were concentrating to your fight, where not only you never disappointed me, but also you broke all the winning records, which I doubt if anybody else in the future will ever break them."

"Apparently, one of the Referees saw you at first, when you went behind the basketball poll and wept. Then from mouth to mouth, every body in the Karate circles new it. So much they were impressed from your emotions, that at every tournament or c/ship we entered, even the spectators were waiting to see you going behind the poll... That's why most of the people were thinking that I was your Son, as nobody in the world will act as emotionally as you did, unless it was for a closed blood relative... But as for your competition winnings: Although you never mentioned to any one, I learned it from my rival competitors that `nobody` will ever get closed to your winning record; so much in KATA (formal exercise) and so much in KUMITE (free fight)...

I also heard it from your very rivals, the Instructors - Sensei, when you used to teach them KUMITE techniques..."

"O.K., O.K.! thank you Son... Although South Africa's Karate is amongst the best in the world, with its Shihan - Sensei to be of the highest in Rank and knowledge outside Japan, they will remember us for a long time. As far as for you are my Son is concern; Dion by now, will spread it all over the Country. We will visit them very soon..."

Reading from the Diary

All of a sudden, right in front of my Jeep, I saw a finger of an animal... no, no, it wasn't an animal but the face of a black man, having on top of his head something like the horns of a buffalo...

"Dead, sorry interrupting you," George said to his Father.

"When I saw the drawing for a first time in South Africa, and without reading the story of course, I thought to myself, that my Sensei had a nightmare when he drew this monster."

"I will tell you for that later, as I did have nightmares for some time..."

He looks at Persa who had lifted her right hand up, like she was in the class - room.

"Yes Persa? Do you want to ask me something?"

"Yes Sensei!" The young girl replied, where contrary to his Son, she calls him Sensei, as she finds it more appropriate at this moment to address him with his Japanese title.

"Athena, which I just embraced her and smelled so nice; what was the reason the Goddess stopped you turning your head back?"

The Master lifts the glass, consuming some juice before answering her question.

"Well Persa, the Goddess, or whoever was with the Goddess face, didn't let me turn my head back, because if I had it turn to see what happened of the explosion, then by now I would be dead! Poisoned by the blown dart...

To assure me that the Goddess was protected me she came the same night into my dream... But let's read from the Diary, because the story is far away from over."

Under Artemis wet eyes, the Master re - opens his Diary with his right hand, again looking through the pages...

The animal – like, was holding with both his hands a poisonous `Blow Dart`, ready to use it with his mouth.

He was exactly in front of the Jeep, in the same line as I was.

For a split of a second our eyes met, and as long as I live I will never forget those eyes; they were red, with burning fire inside their sockets...

I let go only one bullet and I lost him.

I waited for more than 4 minutes until the smock cleared, holding even my breath.

I could see properly now up to 40 meters...

The road was still blocked, but by dead bodies.

Among the dead, I saw two wounded men, moving around their hands, trying to find a weapon (I think)...

Eventually, I looked back.

Quickly I picked up the awful helmet and went behind the second Jeep.

There were most of the men, minus the two Italians, where they were still waiting behind a large tree next to a Hut. Thanks to them, they saved us, throwing the two grenades.

As soon as the men saw me, they all embraced me, except Jean. He was down to his left knee behind the left bumper, holding his face with both of his hands, crying and swearing with pain and anger. His clothes were burned... At that moment the two Italians came running with Gino embraced me. I also thank them for saving us and making the Balumba running.

"Actually the two grenades did the miracle" I said to Gino.

To my question, the men told me that the third grenade I heard was Jean's. When he tried to through it at the Baluba, his hand strike the top of the Jeep's door, thus, dropped it in front of him and exploded, burned him all over; his face as well.

Jean gets up and when he turned towards me, I noticed the damage to his face. He looked like somebody with over 20 burning thick thorns had struck his face, not once, but twice. Only the eyes and eyebrows were intact.

This damn unlucky moment, was not over for Jean, as another deadly incident hit him again, but this time was deadly…

When he was moving left right with pain, we heard a bullet shot and all of a sudden I saw him (we all did) going down like an empty bag.

"Jean!" I shouted and went to him, getting him into my arms, thinking that he was dead.

I checked his pulse and without knowing what and where hit him, I said loudly:

"He is still alive!"

Before even I finished, I heard and saw a bullet striking the ground few centimeters next to my left knee.

"Sharp Shooters, sharp shooters, get cover" I shouted"

They all bent more down except me, as I was holding Jean and both of us were out of the rear of the Jeep, exposing us to the shooter.

I called Jim the Journalist, which incidentally was also wounded in his right arm, with the bullet still inside; to try to nurse Jean, as he didn't have only some medical experience, but he had first - aid kit in his bag as well.

Telling him that, I grabbed his binoculars and when he relieved me from Jean who started coming around… I tried to look by placing the binoculars on top of my mashing gun, with intention to tight them up with my shoe lacers, I noticed that the gun had a fitted binoculars but it was at the side of it.

I clip it on and placed my gun on top of the rear door.

Looking through the binoculars I scan all the possible trees I could see, as deep as possible.

I heard Jean swearing from pain and I turned my face to see where he was hit.

Thanks to the experience and his magic bag, Jim just took out a bottle of morphine and injected Jean, who was screaming with pain once more, but this time he was telling Jim to… kill him.

The bullet may not killed him, but as from this horrible moment, Jean will be a living dead for ever, as the `killing bullet` strike him in between his legs, shattering his organs…

Before I look again to find the sharp shooter, a barrage of bullets, strike the front side of the Jeep, definitely damaged the radiator, possible the engine as well, deprive us to our escape…

While I tried to clear my head of the possible damages of the Jeep, I managed to think that there wasn't any sharp shooter but somebody with a mashing gun, very closed to us.

This time I focused the binoculars to the trees that I thought were closed enough for a mashing gun.

This time I was lucky, I saw the smock, then, I heard the bang on to the Jeep, shattering the left light lens.

I aim calmly, and shoot him… dead, falling from the tree to the ground.

I scan again and again to see if there was anybody else, when I heard Mark calling me, like I was the only one around:

"George, George!"

I turn my head and he was showing me with his finger at the two wounded men where I had I noticed earlier. In fact, he was pointing out the one who was `trying` unsuccessfully to grab a gun next to him, to shoot us…

I looked at the other wounded and appeared to be dead. That made me furious and I exploded at Mark:

"Damn you Mark; can't you see that the man is dying?"

Without paying any attention to him, I went to the front Jeep to make space for Jean and George.

I jump up from the rear door calling Gino to help me to remove all the piping of the Bazooka to the other Jeep and use all possible soft material as a mattress.

When Gino and Carlos (the other Italian) took the pipes, I used some blankets and all our jerseys from our gear, to make it more comfortable for them. Under the circumstances of course!

While on top of the Jeep I look in front of it to see the dead Balumba with the poisonous 'Blow - Dart pipe. He was flat on the ground, facing up, with his buffalo hat still on his head. Apparently, the bullet got him on the forehead in between the eyes.

As I will never forget his red - red eyes, I will also never forget the looks of his face as well!

There, at that moment on top of the Jeep, in the middle of the Jungle of Congo, I made another pledge to God, that:

<When I am out of this bloody war and if is to my power, I will never lift a gun to shoot at any one any more >

Speaking of the devil; when I was ready to jump down of the Jeep, with some tears on my face, I noticed Mark taking his machine - gun, opens its steel legs to full extension and by lying down on the road started shooting at the fatally wounded Balumba, without telling us anything...

He finished all the bullets left in the magazine, without touching him at all.

Then, like a Robot he gets up, throwing his gun on the road and walks towards the Jeep I was in and open the door of the passenger's side. I thought he was going to take one of his forgotten revolvers...

I jump down and went to the same spot behind the Jeep when I was alone fighting for my life.

I bent my left knee, aim carefully to put him out of his misery; had a single shot, praying that was the last one ever...

Before I realized of what happened, Mark first released the hand brake and started the engine...

The Jeep, when I first forced to stop it and swing it to the left, there was a little up hill as most of the roads left and right were, right through all they way to Albertville... thus, when he released the hand – brake, then, the right rear wheel went over my left leg, keeping it trapped on the ground. The pain at first wasn't much, as the American boot protected my ankle.

The men shouted at him to be careful and go back more, but he instead, engaged the first gear and went over it again, making it this time to be very painful.

Mark, pretending of not realizing of what happened, he stops the Jeep at two meters away and gets out shouting at all of us:

"Come on! Come on! Let's get out of this f...p ..."

With the gun in my hands, I got up facing at him with the barrel direct to his flabby belly. I don't know how my eyes looked like, but had some affection on him. He lifted his hands in front of his face asking me to forgive him.

Definitely it wasn't him or my conscious that stopped me, but something more powerful than both; could be my Angel with the face of the Ancient Goddess Athena? Whatever it was, it saved Mark... and in the end it saved me as well!

He was about 2 meters in front.

Without thinking of the pain of my left leg, I moved it forward, turning it left ways to 180 degrees angle, and... back - kicked him (ushiro geri) with the right - rear leg to solar – plexus, forcing him to do, two backward somersaults, striking the dead Baluba, ending up with his face on the ground.

The sudden pivoting on my left leg, made it worse as I twisted and placed a lot of my weight on it.

Ignoring the pain, I went quickly to Jean, where with the help of Gino and Jim, we carried him unconscious to the Jeep, placed him flat on top of the blankets. Using as a pillow all the Jerseys I could find.

Mark on the ground, with some broken ribs, was conscious after all, tried to breath, holding his stomach with great pain.

## CHAPTER TWENTY-ONE

Although the younger of them all, I took charge and placed 7 men to be to the rear Jeep, with Jack driving it and 5 men including myself as a driver, with Mark coming and set next to me, bending his upper body forward, but never the less he is telling me `Sorry` once more.

We started moving with me in the front, having another ordeal to go through. That was, to go over about 50 dead Baluba.

I told Mark and the men at the back to get ready, only to shoot if they see somebody pretending to be dead and trying to shoot us…

With my heart to play basketball inside my chest, I went over the bodies…

When I looked to try to avoid the dead as much as possible, I saw with some relieve, that all of them, apart of guns, they had poisonous Arrows and poisonous Blow Darts, with many flat swords, where were also poisonous at the end as well.

When eventually I entered the ever awful narrow road, I realized that the left front tire not only was flat, but some pieces of it were off, making my driving very difficult.

I looked to see if the other Jeep was following us, because I was worrying about it, as the radiator was damaged and it couldn't be long that the engine will get very hot and burn out…

With out stopping and look back all the time, I somehow managed to drive about 6 kilometers with the first and second gear. During that time, the tire came completely off, thus I was driving for more than 2 kilometers on the rim. We didn't overturn because all the time I kept the Jeep on the left side, where it was higher at most of the road.

I stopped the Jeep, not for the tire, but because the other Jeep did not followed us.

I said to Mark to be useful and help me changed the tire and we must go back, to look for the other men...

I took the Jack and place it under, telling Mark to unscrew the spare wheel.

Before I started lifting the Jeep, I told the men to come out, leaving Jean and George in.

All the men went behind the trees to relieve themselves, enjoying every minute of it, with Jean who just came around, telling me... to kill him!

As for my leg, started complaining at me about neglecting it...

While I am trying to change the tire, thinking to do it fast; so I could attend the other two wounded men as well...

Well, I felt like I was trapped with my own doings, with the only person been responsible to blame was my very stupid - self, as I made everything in this unforgettable adventure to carry me through my mind...

I pulled the wheel out only when Mark gave me the spare, because the Jack wasn't strait, due to the loose rocks underneath it.

I removed the Jack and tight the wheel - nuts.

While I said to Gino to come with me to look for the other men, we heard a bullet shot. From my position I could see with some relieve that the shot was coming from one of our comrades from the other Jeep, who was running, trying to attract our attention by shooting on the air.

The man told me that the engine burned!

We waited for a while for the other 6 men to come and as soon as we were altogether, I took initiative again by telling them a plan I thought while I was changing the tire:

"I think, four of us go back to the Jeep, taking all the fuel of it, all the ammunitions and another spare wheel.

I was explaining the plan to them in English and Greek, while Gino explained it in Italian.

Mark volunteered, so was Gino, also Jim with the bullet still in his arm, and Jack the Sergeant as well.

Four men carefully carried Jean on top of the blanket, with George coming out on his own walking...

I entered the Jeep and started the engine.

Jim, without loosing time, he barraged me with questions about my life, my family and why I went to the Congo etc.

After he promised me that he will never write my really name in the news papers and will never show my picture, I answered all his questions.

Very soon I regret it, because the man risked even his life to write a true and realistic story, taking pictures and movie shots, about the people who also risked their lives to support the Government of Congo. So, later on in Johannesburg, he had a write up story about the others and me.

I am keeping the copy anyway...

"Dad," G.K. interrupts him again. Something that would of never dreamed in the past of doing it, where now comes so natural, making them both smiling.

"Yes Son?" The Father smiled, instead of punishing his student.

"I have seen the newspaper - cutting inside the Diary. In the second year of the ordeal I went with you, when you asked me to clean up your library in Port Elizabeth and the Book was opened. Apart of the write – up, I saw also your drawings and the Congolese money as well…"

"I know, Son. I saw you. I did it on purpose, as it was part of the Psychological tests on you. Among other documents, I left the Diary open, so you could see that I was real, not a spirit, like you went through for 10 years where almost making you losing your mind. The Goddess must have a very good reason of letting you staying that long with the spirits…"

"Spirits?" Mother and Daughter said surprisingly.

The Master looks at Artemis for a few seconds before he continuous:

"You know Artemis, as the Goddess mentioned earlier; our Son lived and practiced for 10 years among the Spirits of our Ancient Ancestors, where all of them were Olympic Champions in their time, becoming Gymnasts later on, teaching their experience to the future Olympic Champions of that Era. Some how the Goddess managed to bring our Son and them together in a secret or possibly a sacred place, teaching him their experience, where in most ways, they aren't very much different to my way, except…"

"Dad, sorry interrupting you again, but, although some of their Philosophy as far as the fighting in general was concern, was very effective and helped me in many ways in and out of the fighting arena… until I met you! Your way, has no equal, as you can turn the individual to be a winning fighting machine, with the ability not only to have the respect of his beaten opponent but to…"

"O.K., O.K. Son", the Master interrupts his student and carries on:

"Let's say, I had the feeling; because what ever I taught you, came out of my heart towards the Son I always wanted to have…"

Artemis interferes, just to take him out off the emotional stress that was going to develop. While talking, she kept holding his hand again:

"You know Giorgo? Into our bad luck, at least you had the pleaser to have our Son with you, even if you didn't known about it. Nevertheless, will you please continue reading from the Diary? How was your leg? Of what I heard while you were reading, it wasn't that bad after all."

"Yes you are right! My leg, although was very uncomfortable, I could bare the pain, but it needed a rest, where at that time I couldn't think of it at all…"

Reading from the Diary

When n we reach the abandon Jeep, the first thing I noticed was the Bazooka still inside…

From that position we were, we could see at least 200 meters back, so we didn't have to let a guard, so, I turned my Jeep, ready to go in case the thousands of Baluba were following us, while I told the men to help me buried the Bazooka in the Jungle, but with my initiative again, we split it in three pieces, buried it in a way of making a triangle. In this way, when hopefully we will reach a base with Soldiers, I could draw them a map, so they could come and collect it…

With a piece of paper, taking it from my Diary (Which was covered with some blood from Jean) I drew a map to the best of my ability under the circumstances.

We took one wheel out and I put it on to my Jeep, thus replaced the one where was damaged. The space for the spare wheel was at the back door of the Jeep.

Also, we took the 20 - litre fuel - container and fixed it at the side of the passenger's door.

Collecting all the ammunitions we could use as well!

I looked at the fuel gauge and I noticed that there was half tank full…where if I had a pipe I could fill-up our fuel tank, as it was also half way full.

At the last moment I thought of something that wasn't to my character but very useful at the time.

I took out my bayonet and told the men to give me their helmets and nobody must smock.

Lying under the Jeep, and with the third effort I made a hall under the petrol tank, then, by using my own helmet and the others as well, I collected the precious fluid.

By this way I managed to collect about 25 litres.

Now, how many litres went inside the tank of our Jeep; that was up to Gino who was already dizzy from pouring into the fuel - tank. I escaped dizziness because half way I let Mark to come under the Jeep, as he wouldn't mind, because drunkenness was his game!

While I was under, I couldn't help thinking of the damaged cars I saw in the Villages.

Because, they couldn't be taken out of the country, the cars could be damaged by they very owners and not by the Cannibals-Balumba, so in this way nobody will take the benefit out of them anymore. Not even the regular Army…

The whole `operation` lasted about 40 minutes.

When we returned back, our comrades welcomed us like we were Heroes.

"Shihan," asked Persa."Why you are calling them Cannibals? Were they really Men - Eaters?"

"Unfortunately Persa, they were! I cannot tell you if all of the Balumba were Cannibals, but as horrible as it sounds, yes, I came across at least three incidents, where Balumba ate parts of the bodies of white men!"

Reading from the Diary again

During our absent, the men left behind were useful by cutting many flat leaves and made more comfortable bed than the blankets for our wounded man.

Now we had to go through of another ordeal, which looked like an action movie, with me as a Producer, Director and Actor...

First we took all the leaves and blankets back to the Jeep, carrying Jean... When I was trying to place some of our gear around him, I felt his arm grabbing my leg. I brought my face close to his and he told me to kill him...

"Please George!" Jean repeats. "Please kill me!"

I saw the pain in his eyes, but it wasn't only from the wound, but from his Psychological feelings of loosing his manhood.

<Of what I promised him, I meant everything I said up to the last word>

"Jean, I can't do it! I am not that strong as you think I am. But I can promise you this: As long as you keep your hopes high, I will do everything it takes to drive you to the hospital, even if I have to transport you on top of an Elephant. Please, do not lose hope, as there is a possibility that you can be cured!"

With out waiting for an answer, I spoke to George who was sitting patiently next to him to look after Jean and at the same time I took away all possible sharp things including his bayonet.

The time I jumped down of the Jeep, I felt a sharp pain on my leg, which looked like somebody stamp me with a sharp burning knife on the right side of my ankle.

Jim, who was near, saw me and asked me to take off my boot.

I sat on top of the open rear door of the Jeep and Jim went down to his left knee undone my bootlaces, taking off my left boot.

Some men gathered around to see what was going on, because I suddenly realized, that these people were relying heavily on me!

After he examined it, pressing his fingers all over the ankle, he said that it wasn't fractured, but needed a rest.

"Sensei, I mean Dad! Now that you are expert in this kind of injury, what do you think about Jim's way towards your leg?"

"Well, first of all, of what I know now Jim didn't know then, so lets giving some credit for that, but under the circumstances and without ice, he did an excellent job. Lucky he had an elastic bandage, but he tight it more tight than should be, and very wisely told me not to drive anymore…His human interest to help me with my injured leg, it turned to his benefit, because while he was working at it, I noticed that from time to time, he was grinning with pain, touching his wounded arm:"

"Jim, I said. Isn't dangerous for your arm to have the bullet more than two hours into your system? Could have some poison on it? You know that, almost all Baluba are having poison all over their hands. The bullet inside your arm, I think it should come out immediately! I was giving advice without exactly knowing how about poison was really working, as there were so many different kinds."

## CHAPTER TWENTY-TWO
### Reading again from the Diary

"If I am going to write into my Diary all the experience I went through in the last ten minutes, I may just needed another book to fill up"

As I convinced Jim to remove the bullet immediately out! He convinced me to do it. And so I did…

Jim was sitting at the same place I was earlier when he nursed my leg.

With my assistance, he removed his military shirt, exposing his wounded arm. Continue he opens his Magic bag, taking out a surgical knife - looking instrument.

When he took it out of its plastic bag, it shines under the Sun who had the audacity to come through the thick trees this time of the morning, to dry our dump body in this cursed Jungle.

Apart of that instrument, also he took out a tweezers with 45 degrees angle, giving them both to me. Carried on, he took out a small plastic bottle containing white spirit and a sterilize cotton. He opened the cap of the spirit and squeezes a lot of it on to the cotton. He then takes the two instruments from me and cleans them up. From another half of the cotton he cleans my hands, then, he turned the cotton inside - out and cleaned his wound.

Now I can see it clearly from the dry blood that was on it. Around the wound it was getting black and it started swollen up…

He digs once more in to his bag and takes out a large sterilized bandage, imbue it with iodine and penicillin.

After all this ceremony - like, he seats on the ground and he lifts his arm, resting it on top of the opened door of the Jeep, in front of my face.

"I haven't done it before!" I said loudly, in case somebody of the men, who gathered around us, could take my place.

"I couldn't trust anyone else!" Jim said calmly...

After few seconds of hesitation, I decided to do it, because of the wound was still in front of me and I didn't like the color of it.

"Jim I will do it providing you take something for the pain."

"I have only one bottle of morphine left and I will inject it to Jean later on when he is in pain (Jean was a sleep again), but I will drink some whisky."

He then dugs in his bag again with his free hand and Gino helps him to open it.

In the bottle I could see that was very little left. He opens his mouth but to close it again without touching it. He then removes his own belt and before he bites it he tells me to keep what was left from the whisky for Jean, because he will need it when the Morphine is finished."

What could I say for this man?

I said to Gino to open the bottle of the white spirit and I cleaned my hands once more; also helped him to clean his hands, as I wanted to use him to hold the tweezers.

Using my fingers of my left hand, I pressed gently around the wound, thus, I felt where and how deep the bullet should be.

As we had no other cotton to wipe the blood while I will open it, I said to Gino to use the one who had cleaned our hands and tools, but he mustn't touch the wound its self, because of the spirit been dirty from our hands...

# George Karavidas, G.K.

This first time of my life that I attended a real wound, I felt the need of becoming a Surgeon or a Doctor as such.

I rested my elbow next to Jim's hand, so to be steady, and taking a deep breath I made a cut of two centimeters; first from the bottom of the wound. While Gino was cleaning it up, I quickly made the same cut from the top of the wound. With out loosing time, with Jim grinning with pain still biting his belt, I grabbed the tweezers from Gino's hand. Then, while I pushed into the wound, I opened it to about a centimeter and quickly pushed it again. When I closed it, I felt that I am catching the bullet. Still holding my breath, I pulled out the tweezers with the bullet in its grip.

I still remember my triumph:

I lifted the tweezers with the bullet in it, shouting like a little child that just had won a toy. All the men did the same, except Gino, who shouted at me to cover the wound with the bandage. As for Jim, he spitted out his belt, screaming, not of course from happiness but with a great pain.

Before I used the proper bandage I said to Jim, that I am going to throw some of the spirit on the wound to make sure that was clean before I will bandage it.

Jim screams a little but he sustains it...

Quickly I started using the bandage carefully so the penicillin will go direct to the wound, so, to relieve Jim from pain.

By taking his belt from the ground, I click it making a temporary sling and place it around his neck, telling him to rest his hand on it.

To ease his pain a little I tried to make a jock:

"You know Jim; the wound has to be stitched. If you have anything of that staff in your magic bag, then I will do it for you, as now I have some experience, using you as an experimental animal."

We both laughed, making Jim to ease up his pain, as this man was an exception of the rule...

After few minutes, I noticed that Jim was shivering with fever and I could see the pain reached its climax.

Although I was expecting his answer, I asked him again to use the morphine, as the penicillin maybe didn't penetrated the wound...

When he said, No! I looked inside his bag and find a packet of aspirins. I took two and his canteen where was also in the bag, I gave them to him, one by one. He placed his strong arm around me and said:

"Thank you Greek! I clean forgot the aspirins. You know that, if we get out of here and I go back to the States, I can recommend you to a few Universities, in case you want to become a Surgeon - Doctor.

"You know Jim, while I was attending your wound; the same thought came through into my mind."

I helped him to seat opposite George, having Jean (who was lying flat and still a sleep) in between them.

In a few minutes the three of them were sleeping.

We were 12 men, with the three wounded occupying 40% of the Jeep, plus our gear, our guns and ammunitions, of another 30%.

I had to place two of the men on top of the flat bonnet...

I gave Mark, who was sitting again next to me, all our mashing guns to keep them at his feet, in a manner that we could take them out easy.

In this way, I gave the 7 men some space, so they will not touch the wounded.

I didn't do anything about Georges wound, as he was sleeping all the time from the sleeping tablets where Jim had given him during our journey, while he cleaned his wound and bandaged it as well.

The Master stopped reading and said to Artemis:

"Although I will never forget everything I went through in the Congo, this particular ride I will remember it like it happened only yesterday. But, I better read through the Diary where I only wrote few important things that I thought was necessary…"

Reading from the Dairy again

I took the steering, while the two men climbed on the boot. They were both swearing; one was swearing in English and the other in Italian.

Also with three wounded men urgent needed medical attention, plus 7 men squashed, holding the bars of the Jeep, trying not to touch the wounded, I engaged the first gear going where? Thank God there was only one road!

As for Mark, who was sitting next to me, he was breathing heavily and swearing inside his false teach, because all the machine guns were with their barrels facing up to his face, also some belts full of bullets in between them, made his life more miserable than already was!

All of us men, including Mark, Jean and Jack, we had one thing in common:

We all regretted the time we signed up to come to this part of Africa, longing to go back to the South, like it was our own Country (with the exception of Mark and Jack where were born in South Africa).

Although the returning road was the same to one of whom we went to Albertville, it wasn't the same, as I was doing the driving from the other side of it.

Fortunately from the start, I had the wisest idea of wearing my helmet, as I did not only bent my head to the left, out of the Jeep, but also my body as well; because of the two men on the boot, I couldn't see properly.

In this way, the helmet helped me to avoid even fatal injury to my eyes and face…

Now that I did the driving slower than before, I noticed the small amateur made bridges we went through, how dangerous could be, not only to break and taking us down with them, but if the Balumba had the brain of a child, they could easy dismantled it a little and waited for us there, to kill as all, as we would be trapped…

As I remember, I did the same thought while we were going down to Albertville as well…

My thoughts were interrupted by a sharp up hill road, which was still of course narrow and gravel.

As soon as I reached the highest point, I heard Jean again, telling me to kill him!

He was in great pain!

George, who was next to him, told me in Greek while he was showing me some blood on his fingers:

"I think Jean is bleeding."

Before I said anything, Jim came about and told me to stop!

By the looks of it, the penicillin and the two aspirins did their work and of what I could see the fever must of have subside.

I find an opening and slowly applied the breaks.

As soon as I jumped out of the Jeep, I started doing some stretching exercises, ignoring the pain of my leg, which was still swollen up.

In spite of the condition of my leg, I will keep on driving until we find a camp or a hospital, because I promised it to Jean.

With Jim's permission, I opened his bag, taking two aspirins. I couldn't find water and when I turned my head to ask Jim of what happened to his canteen, I saw the water-canister in front of my face, coming from Jim's good arm:

"Here you are, future Surgeon," Jim said. Meaning every word!

My life in the Hell of Congo continues.

With the two aspirins in my mouth and the bottle in my hands...I heard, and then I saw a truck coming up the hill towards us.

Without thinking, I drop the canister inside the bag, then, I run and grab one machine gun under the open eyes and mouth of Mark, I shouted at him and to the men to grab their guns, while I took cover behind the Jeep. The least I could do was to protect the wounded men first.

Mark and the rest froze on their seats.

The truck with two men in front and about 40 men on top, stopped next to us...

With the greatest of pleaser and relief, all men were regular soldiers with their captain seating next to the driver.

When they saw us, they lifted their guns saluting us like we were Heroes

Apart of the Captain, I noticed... oh ...thank God, there was a black Doctor with his assistance, which was a young boy of about 16 years old.

That 16 - year boy - nurse, before even come down of the truck, had a good look at Jean who was lying inside the Jeep. He jumped down carrying with his hands two white steel boxes, with a red cross on them.

While the boy was coming to see Jean and the rest of the wounded, shouted something at the Doctor, showing him the Jeep.

When the Doctor tried to climb up the Jeep from the open back door, Jean, instead of appreciating the fact, that a Doctor was found in the middle of the Jungle to clean up his wound, to give him proper medication, because morphine was not medication but drug… he kicked him to his chest instead, forcing him to get out of the Jeep, falling flat on his back.

Luckily that no one of the soldiers, neither the Captain saw the Doctor been kicked.

The Soldiers run to help him getting up, thinking that he slipped down by himself. While the Doctor dusted his white coat, Jean tried to get hold of his gun from his belt, where thanks the stupidity of me and Mark, had it with him all the time…

I grabbed his arm. When he realized he had no power to get it away from my hand, tried unsuccessfully to bit it. Then he burst into tears, telling me something that shook me to my roots:

"The Balumba not only killed my parents, but my wife and my two children, smashed their bodies on a tree and eat them in front of my wife. Did the same to her later as well"

For a moment, I was going to let him grab his pistol and not only let him shoot anything that was black, but I was going to do the same thing with my machine gun as well.

Nothing happened of course, because the brave and understanding Doctor came closer to us. With tears in his eyes (not from the kick he received from Jean) and with perfect English, said to the Belgian, like he new his ordeal. His voice was loud and clear:

"The Balumba killed my wife and my three children. The fourth one was saved, because he was at school at the Mission with the Belgian Monks... That's him!" The Doctor pointed out at his young assistant.

"I am so afraid about his life, that I do not send him to school any more... and he wants to be a Doctor..."

In the end, Jean wasn't convinced, but agreed to his medical advice from

outside of the Jeep, using Jim and me as the Doctors hands.

Jim had a brilliant idea. After exchanging glances with the Doctor, then the assistant nurse gave Jim a bottle to inject Jean.

After few minutes Jean was fast a sleep, thus, we didn't have to leave the Jeep for the Doctor to attend our wounds as well, as he climbed up and went to Jean first.

With my help, we took Jeans clothes off, and for a first time I saw the horrible wound. The bullet went through his organs, but didn't strike the spine colon, only scratched it, which means that there wasn't any danger of becoming paralyzed.

The Doctor cleaned it with wet bandages, which was given to him by his Son.

While he was nursing Jean, he examined him thoroughly, with his Son next to him, asking questions all the time.

George the Belgium, welcome the Doctor and his Son, as nobody of us paid a really attention to his open wound.

First, the Doctor injected the wound for the pain, and then stitched it with the stitched machine he Son gave him.

Straightaway he cleaned again and stitched Jims arm. While his Son was bandaging it, Jim said to the Doctor that I was the one who took the bullet out.

"You did a good Job my friend," the Doctor said. "Now let's take a look at your leg!"

While the Doctor was examining my ankle, I told Jim a jock that came to my mind while I was going to open his wound:

"When you put the bottle into your mouth to drink and you didn't do it after all; I thought of taking the bottle and finished it myself, as I needed the carriage to do it. When I finally reject it as well, I laughed, thinking of the old Cow Boy movies when `the Doctor` (by fluke) was always drunk; and instead of giving the whisky to the patient he drank it by himself…"

"You need also to go to the hospital, for casting your leg," said the Doctor smiling.

"How far is the hospital from here Doc?" I said, smiling too.

"It will be close to 6 hours with the truck. It is a temporary hospital, which consists of some volunteered Doctors and Journalists. All the Journalists have Medical knowledge.

"You know Doc. when you were coming up with the truck, I swollen 2 aspirins, with out any water and…"

"I saw you! I was on top of the truck when you run and grab the machine gun, taking cover behind the Jeep.

We thought you were going to shoot us... Here, drink this! It is chocolate milk."

The Doctor also told me, not to drive and `give it a rest`.

"Doctor, so much of my stomach and my leg, we thank you! I also thank you on behalf of the other wounded men as well... oh boy," I said surprisingly, as I looked at the men and all three were fast a sleep!

Now where all were a sleep, I dare to ask the Doctor about Jean's condition:

"Doc, will Jean be normal again?"

"As for his manhood, I cannot tell you yet. But definitely he cannot have children any more!"

I looked up, facing God, begging him to be merciful on Jean's case:

"Please God," I said loudly. "Let Jean have at least one child, as he lost all his family..."

"He can adopt!" Was the answer of the young black boy, who had the desire of becoming a Doctor!

Another two comic - tragic incidents happened again in the middle of the Jungle

While the Doctor attended our wounds, Mark and the Captain, made themselves useful and told our men and the soldiers to cut more flat leaves, carried them on top of the truck, making a soft double mattress, which even Tarzan would envy it for his Jungle mate, Jane.

The soldiers carefully carried the three sleeping men and placed them on top of the leaves.

Then, the Doctor told them to carry me as well, but even before finished his command, I was on top already, telling him:

"Thanks Doc!"

Here, on top of the truck, I was ready to take some time to write on the bloody but in good order Diary of mine; where two funny things happened, and from where ever angle I tried to look at them, I couldn't laugh, as they weren't funny at all.

The first was, when all of a sudden I saw Sof climbing up into the truck, with bandages on his left knee.

When I questioned him of what happened, he said that, when we were at the hotel, a bullet, by slinging on the road strike him on his knee and slung again with out penetrating his bone.

While he was telling me all these rubbish, avoided looking at me, but he looked at George who was just coming around:

"You see! It's about time that I also have some luck, like you three had..."

I was going to call him a coward, but thinking of the ordeal he went through when he was dropped out of the Jeep; I pretended to be busy writing in my Diary.

Just as well, the Doctor appeared, telling me to explain to Sof that he shouldn't be on the truck among the wounded...

"It's O.K. Doc, I will tell him, but if it's all right with you, I suggest that he can stay up here, in case I need him to help me with the wounded."

While I was explaining to Sof of what I just said to the Doctor, he grabbed my hand and tried unsuccessfully to kiss it...

As for the second: Jean, was awake all the time (but not in pain) well before they carried him to the truck, but he kept his eyes closed, as he didn't want to see who carried him...

Anyway, he grabs my sleeve and tells me to call the fu…black nurse to bring toilette paper, as he has just done it, inside his pants.

I believed him, because when I looked at him in surprise, I saw that he just had his last … bowl

Without the swearing word, I repeat it to the Doctor, where apparently he new that Jean was awake all the time…

"We must clean him first!"

The Doctor naturally would ask his Son to do all the dirty work!

He calls his Son and tells him to climb up:

"If it's O.K. by him," said the Doctor, pointing out at Jean.

I looked at him and he said:

"If the boy comes alone, then it's O.K."

I caress Jean's swollen cheek, while I was telling the boy:

"It will be much better if you bring him some pampers as well."

Although I said it as a jock, the 16 years youth but experience Boy-Nurse, took it very serious (like a Father like a Son) and after only few minutes of leaving the truck, came back with three home made pampers, made by using some thick bandages, fixing them so well, that even Jean gave him a smile of appreciation.

The boy told me to empty the pockets of Jeans trousers and take it off together with his underpants and give them to him. I did it and he threw them inside a plastic bag that had it with him, telling his Father in English to bring him another trousers. The Doctor in turn, shouted at the Captain…

While we were waiting for the Doctor, Jim and I cleaned Jean out of all his dirt, leaving the boy out of this mess.

When Jean was ready to put his pampers on, which they were fixed in a manner that covered his wound as well, then, I took a bullet out of my belt and closed it in one of my hands, telling Jim to pick one of my closed fists:

"Jim, the unlucky one, will put on the pumper - underpants to Jean. Take your pick!"

I did all this to enlighten the situation at this time of so much pain and stress.

Jim, who understood my point, picked the one I had the bullet, but because of his wound I helped him cover Jean's bottom. At the same moment a colorful camouflage pair of trousers landed next to the boy from his Fathers arms.

The boy took it and with a smile gave it to me, where again with the help of Jim's good hand I put it on to Jean, trying not to pull it high and irritate his wound.

It was Sof this time, pulling my sleeve:

"George! Tell the Doctor to give me some aspirins for my knee."

I don't know how I looked at him, but since then, he never bother me again any more, about any form of painkiller!

The Boy took the plastic bag with all the bloody clothes and everything else inside, and by telling us goodbye jumped down in to his Fathers arms.

The Father took the bag and gave it to a soldier to burn it.

I thank Father and Son once more, and before they leave, I grabbed my black book, asked him to tell me his name and his Sons as well, so to write them into my private Diary.

The black Doctor puts his arm around his Son's shoulder and walks away with him.

After about few meters, he turns, and while smiles exposing his healthy white teeth, tells me:

"Call me Doc! As for my Son... call him `The Doctors Son`."

And by both lifting their hands up waving at us, they walk a way into the Jungle, followed by the Captain and all the soldiers, except one who will drive the track to the nearest temporary hospital, which will be about five and a half hours drive...

There is more to it as the adventure in the hell of the Congo is far from over yet!

George Karavidas (G K) Email: sktp@hol.gr

The 20th/21st Century modern Art of SHOTOKOUNTHIGH (SKTP) as it is up to day (Roots and Philosophy of Ancient Pagration 648 B. c.).

The scientific SKTP is not made for anyone who wants to pass his time, but only to those that want self respect and respect for others. The SKTP Black Belt `Karateka` has to pass difficult (but not impossible) tasks that will mark his life forever (Male or Female, Young or Old). The Art is not for showing off (when one can do almost impossible fits), never looks for trouble, never swears, respects his parents and the older, never beats his younger brother, never touches drugs, he lives by law, he never fears or underestimates his opponent in and out of the fighting arena. As long as he is following the path that has been drawn and taught by Grand Master George Karavidas will soon realize the importance of learning the above Art; not only will get the benefit of staying alive when needed and win in tournaments and competitions in general, but will get the pleasure out of it by always trying to improve himself in all situations of life. The Philosophy of all happenings that are so attracted by all, lying in the following syllabuses created by the above Grand Master where he brought up to surface the Roots and Philosophy of the Ancient Gymnasts and the Elite Pagratiates, with his own Philosophy, to suit the modern world of Martial Arts and specially to Karate, without copy NO ONE.

`MY PHILOSOPHY of the 14 SYLLABUSES of my ART`

SSHARPNESS
HHARDNESS
OOBJECTIVENESS (OBJECTIVITY)

T TOUGHNESS
OOFFENSIVENESS
KKNOWLEDGE
OOCELOT
UUNEXPECTED
NNIMBLE
TTHOUGHTFUL
HHARMONIC
IINCOMPARABLE
G GENUINE
HHIGH SPIRITED

`Via SHARPNESS and HARDNESS comes the development of OFFENSIVENESS, but only through TOUGHNESS directs your KNOWLEDGE who lights up the OBJECTIVITY of an attack. Then, UNEXPECTED by been OFFENSIVE with OCELOTS - NIMBLE movements, makes you INCOMPARABLE because you are GENUINE through HARMONY and HIGH - SPIRITED`

My PHILOSOPHY of been EFFECTIVE in FIGHTING(With or Without Rules)

DIRECT MOVE
(In Attack - Defense - Retaliation)

ECONOMY OF SPEED
(Zero inactivity - Zero time to Target)

PERFECT BALANCE
(When strike Opponent - When block Opponent's attack -When missing target in attack or retaliation - When blocked by Opponent)

KNOWLEDGE

(In ability to react and perform effectively when needed)

PERFECT Co - Operation between MIND/BODY & BODY/MIND.

Analyzing the above in some detail, the reader will soon realize what makes SKTP Unique and Genuine, worth of devoting ones life and pass it on to their children.

The SKTP writes a long time student from the Island of Samos (Now a Monk in the Holly Mountain of `Athos` devoting his life to God):

`It is the road to find the unknown. It is a continuation of our inner adventure, a non-stop fight with the most difficult adversary and with the only Judge, the deeper one self. The SKTP is a non-stop investigation-way to perfection, with out end; only the road ahead with the willpower that drives you to the limits, with unbridled courage hoping to reach the highest. It is worth to the contemporary human to dare this adventurous fascinating trip: The road to SHOTOKOUNTHIGH INTERNATIONAL (Roots+Phylosophy of Ancient Pagratio 648 B. c.) to feel the unlimited excitements and deep satisfaction of ones soul, that is when he discovers that all his expectations are before him, as long as he is following the path`

THE SHOTOKOUNTHIGH – PAGRATIO DEMANDS

The above Art of fighting demands from the practitioner who has the courage and the ability to carry on the above Art, because gives him unlimited Knowledge. Yes, the SKTP defers from other Styles, but at the same time is geared by its Creator to compete with all Karate Styles or Systems. Demands (apart of the practitioner) from the Parents, and from the Present and future Instructors, to understand that the Art, as not only educates but cultivates the body, thus, the Ancient and the Present well known Athletes of all sports had it as a motto in their lives which is `Healthy Mind in Healthy Body`.

To reach the ultimate of `Healthy Mind in Healthy Body` is not that easy, thus, the practitioner has to go through 3 Bio Psychological stages:

## THE STAGE OF NATURAL DEVELOPMENT

Improvement of biological strength
Cultivation of kinesiology
Spiritual and soul balance

## THE STAGE OF BROUGHT UP

Social
Moral attitude
Standard of values

## THE STAGE OF DISCIPLINE

Self control
Confidence
Self – Respect
Meditation
Tranquility

"Where ever you are, one day you may become a colorful National or International Champion and false fully you think you are somebody, but with a good character and very high discipline, you KNOW that you are Somebody"

Grand MasterGEORGE KARAVIDAS